"I need the bakery to succeed for my children. They need a safe, permanent home."

Tam's gaze flickered. "I get it. And I wish you luck," she said.

"Thanks. I think."

She pointed toward her herb shop and the empty real estate beside it. "Do you see that space there? I've been wanting to sell my own teas for years, and Petals and Pie is the perfect way. It's going to be a meeting place, the heart of the town, I hope. It'd make my daughter and me more comfortable, that's for sure."

Patrick's chest tangled with emotions. A tea and pie room across from a bakery. He would have to do more than repaint. He'd need it to be irresistible. Patrick realized Tam could see the calculations in his eyes and cleared his throat. "I better head over to the school and get Scarlet," he mumbled.

"I'm right behind you," she echoed in a companionable tone as she climbed into her car.

Yes. Yes, you are, he thought in exasperation.

Danielle Thorne is a Southern girl who treasures home and family. Besides books, she loves travel, history, cookies and naps. She's eternally thankful for the women she calls friends. Danielle is the author of over a dozen novels with elements of romance, adventure and faith. You'll often find her in the mountains or at the beach. She currently lives south of Atlanta with her sweetheart of thirty years and two cats.

Books by Danielle Thorne

Love Inspired

His Daughter's Prayer
A Promise for His Daughter
A Home for the Twins
The Doctor's Christmas Dilemma
The Beekeeper Next Door
A Guardian Till Christmas
Winning Over the Baker

Visit the Author Profile page at LoveInspired.com for more titles.

WINNING OVER THE BAKER

DANIELLE THORNE

LOVE INSPIRED
INSPIRATIONAL ROMANCE

LOVE INSPIRED®
INSPIRATIONAL ROMANCE

ISBN-13: 978-1-335-93192-4

Winning Over the Baker

Recycling programs for this product may not exist in your area.

Love Inspired
22 Adelaide St. West, 41st Floor
Toronto, Ontario M5H 4E3, Canada
www.LoveInspired.com

Printed in Lithuania

MIX
Paper | Supporting responsible forestry
FSC® C021394

A friend loveth at all times.
                —*Proverbs* 17:17

For Tamara with love.

Chapter One

Patrick Butler slid a mixing bowl into the antiquated chiller just as the baby began to cry in the back office. He glanced at the clock over the commercial sink in The Last Re-Torte Bakery's kitchen. The oven timer let out a tired, screeching sound, and he hurried to take out a sheet of macadamia cookies before they burned. Little Jax began to wail. Patrick set the hot pan on the counter beside his last batch of peach hand pies and darted to where the eight-month-old had been napping.

Giant tears coursed down Jax's cheeks. Patrick scooped him up. "Jaxon Timothy," he murmured, patting the little boy to comfort him. A wave of love rushed through him although Jax wasn't his own. Only a few weeks after taking Jax in, Patrick and the baby had bonded like two souls adrift at sea, and adoption had been the next step. But twelve-year-old Scarlet? His relationship with his daughter was a shipwreck.

Patrick pressed Jax into his chest. Tiny fingers clutched at his shirt, and the wails subsided. He wondered if rushing to the baby's side every time he cried made him insecure, but Patrick's godmother, Donna, had assured Patrick doing so gave Jax the attention he needed.

Jax sighed with contentment, and Patrick dismissed the concern. He changed the baby's diaper and slid Jax into a baby carrier to ride piggyback. It was the only way, Patrick thought, feeling a little ridiculous as he returned to the bakery kitchen to transfer the cookies onto a cooling rack. He had to get familiar with The Last Re-Torte before Donna quit the bakery business for good. With a diagnosis of rheumatoid arthritis, she couldn't do much in addition to caring for a home and grandchildren who needed her.

As if hearing his thoughts, Donna appeared, silver hair loose in its bun. "It's one o'clock. I have to head to the dentist, then pick up my granddaughters from school," she reminded him. "I'll leave the register open. It shouldn't get too busy."

Patrick nodded. "Sure, no problem. Give me five minutes." Donna's daughter, Gretchen, was like a sister to him. She only helped out on occasion at the family bakery because she had three children of her own to wrangle. He knew the kids needed their grandmother, and it was fine. Besides, he looked forward to working in the front of the store for a bit because his shoulders ached.

Donna tickled Jax on the chin with slender fingers as he grasped at the icing bowl. She appeared thinner than Patrick had ever seen. "You'll hear the front door bells." She hesitated. "Are you doing okay, Patrick? You haven't had time to rest since you got in last Thursday."

"I slept some last night." Patrick didn't add that Jax hadn't slept through the night. "I'll catch up later. It was important to take Scarlet shopping before registering her at the school."

"Do you want me to pick her up today?"

The ache in Patrick's back deepened. "I better do it. She still hates me, or so she reminded me this morning when I made her ride the bus on her first day."

Donna chuckled. "It's just a phase, and there's only six weeks of school left. She'll be okay."

"I hope so," mumbled Patrick. How many young girls were thrust into the arms of a father they'd never been allowed to see on top of starting a new school in late spring? "I just want her to meet some kids before next fall."

"I think that's smart." Donna picked up her purse and left, leaving Patrick alone to watch the store after the lunch crowd returned to work. She was so sweet, so godly, she couldn't fathom what Scarlet had endured in her short life. Unbeknownst to him, the girl had been exposed to appalling situations while her mother became addicted to drugs. No wonder she despised him.

Jax whimpered, so Patrick gave him a broken cookie to nibble, then took the dishes to the sink and started the water. The front door bells jingled. He turned off the tap and grabbed a hand towel, then hurried to the register, trying not to notice the cheerful but fading pink-and-turquoise decor that reminded him of an old Florida hotel lobby. The store had deteriorated during the past year along with Donna's health.

An athletic woman with bobbed hair straightened from over a bread case. "Hi," she called in a sunny voice. "Is Donna here?"

Patrick's cheeks pulled into a smile, and he rested his hands on the counter. "I'm afraid not."

She put a hand on her hip, brunette brows rising over the roundest sapphire eyes he'd ever seen. They complemented her lightly freckled cheeks. Her short hair, another cool shade of brown, reminded him of dark caramel, and it fluttered when she swung her chin in surprise. "You're kidding."

"I'm not. She just left."

"Hmm." She glanced out the window on the way to meet him at the register. "I was hoping to get some peaches."

"Peach pie?" asked Patrick.

"No, actual peaches from her orchard."

"They're not quite ready yet."

"I mean when they are if she doesn't have anymore."

"I just finished hand pies with some of last year's crop that she canned. Would you like one?"

"I need them for a tea recipe. I dehydrate them."

"Oh." Patrick understood now. "I'm afraid they won't be for sale." Donna had promised him this year's crop. His mini pies were famous at his former restaurant, even among the employees. "I'm hoping hand pies will bring in customers who just want a quick snack," he explained.

"That's not a bad idea," she murmured, glancing past him to the back with a look of concern.

"I like to use what's in season," he added, hoping she understood.

"So do I. Oh—I'm Tam," she added. "Tamara Rochester. I own The Gracious Earth herb shop across the street. I'm going to open a tea room next door to the shop this summer. And I need the peaches for one of my teas I want to stock along with the pies and pastries."

Patrick extended a hand. "Patrick Butler. I'm buying the bakery, and Donna is my godmother."

He might as well have said he was an alien. Tam's cheerful smile dropped off her face so fast he thought he heard it hit the floor. "Buying? I thought The Last Re-Torte was closing."

He shook his head. "She was going to close then she offered it to me because... I was looking for something. We decided to keep it quiet until I got here."

Tam gaped as if processing the news was difficult. "Well, that's a surprise. Especially since my tearoom will sell pies and pastries, too."

Patrick's heart dropped. "Is that so?" A second pastry place in town? With pies? He was a dreamer, a doer, not a savvy businessman.

"Yes."

Jax gurgled, and Tam's eyes widened. Patrick twisted around so she could see the baby. "This is Jax."

"Aw. Hi, little guy," murmured Tam. She leaned over the counter and tickled a foot. Jax giggled. "It's wonderful you can bring him to work."

Patrick searched her eyes and saw sincerity, despite that she had been counting on the bakery closing. It made him feel like he was doing something right. It also relieved some of the guilt Scarlet had dealt out at breakfast before she stomped out to the bus. *You love him more than me, and he's not even yours!*

"Are you new to Lagrasse?"

"I'm from Miami. And yes, as soon as I get settled and the paperwork goes through, I'll be the owner. Donna and my mom were best friends, and my mom passed so..." *I need a home for these children.* He released a weighted breath. "Donna is like a second mother to me."

"I'm sorry about your mom."

Patrick nodded his appreciation. "The rest of my family's in Boston so I'm staying with Donna until I can get our own place." He needed his application for the loan to go through and to get the bakery back on its feet first, but he kept that to himself.

"She's generous," Tam observed. "She always sells me peaches in the spring."

Feeling a little selfish, Patrick leaned forward. "Look, I need the entire crop. I like to freeze the surplus."

The entrepreneur across from him grimaced.

"I guess I better let you get busy then." Tam had lost her smile.

"Are you sure you don't want to try a hand pie?"

"No, I—" She reached into her purse as if she'd changed her mind. "Yes, but I'll pay."

Patrick hurried to the kitchen juggling Jax in his arms. After wrapping a hand pie in a piece of wax paper, he returned to the front, where she waved a debit card. "I think you'll like it since you're a peach girl," he said. He bagged the pastry with one clumsy hand.

Tam inserted her payment into the card reader. "Oh, I'm a peach alright, and a good judge of pie."

Patrick sat Jax on the counter between them and met her challenging gaze. "I was born in Valdosta and have ten years' experience in the restaurant business. Donna believes in me. She was my first mentor, and I'm going to bring this old place back to life for her."

Tam examined him as if sizing him up. Jax reached for her carryout bag, but Patrick intervened and handed it to her. "Let me know what you think."

"Don't worry. I will." She sounded serious, but she gave the baby a gentle shake on the hand with hers.

Her ring finger was bare, Patrick noticed. Curiosity bubbled up inside him until she gave him a polite wave and sailed out the door. Clutching Jax to keep him safe on the counter, Patrick seesawed between concern and interest despite the layers of barnacles on his heart. He needed the peaches for the bakery, and he needed the bakery to be successful so he could settle down and heal his broken family—what was left of it. It'd probably be best if he avoided the herb shop owner across the street, especially if she thought The Last Re-Torte staying open was a problem for her new tea and pie place. Unaware of the hiccup in his father's plans, Jax flapped at the front door where Tam had disappeared as if calling her back.

* * *

Early the next morning, Tam Rochester saw a sign for summer enrichment classes as she pulled into Lagrasse Middle School. It was a reminder the school year would soon be over, and her daughter, Piper, would be an eighth grader in the fall. Next would be high school then her dream college in Athens, Georgia. Tam's shoulders sagged. Her only child would leave home in a few years. It hurt her heart, and to be honest, her wallet. The Gracious Earth only broke even these days, and it was time to get serious about saving for college to secure Piper's future. That was the motivation behind the tearoom she'd planned, but the news the bakery wasn't closing now had mucked up her vision.

"Bye, Mom!" Piper grabbed her backpack and reached for the door handle.

"Remember who you are and that you're loved." It was Tam's customary farewell.

"Okay, Mom. You, too." Piper pushed open the passenger door open and jumped out, her shoulder-length ponytail bobbing as she skipped off to join a group of girls in jeans and short-sleeved shirts. Tam watched until they disappeared into the school, then wistfully pulled back out onto the rural highway lined with cars heading into Lagrasse. She marveled at ribbons of morning sunlight crowning the tall Georgia pines as she headed the other direction. They bordered fields of young peanuts and corn that would be replaced by soybeans after an early harvest.

She knew what it was like to be replaced. Her ex had left them before Piper turned two. Ruminating over bittersweet memories of her young family before her dreams were shattered, Tam slowed as she approached a row of spindly mailboxes. Donna Olsen's farmhouse stood outside Lagrasse's limits, surrounded by a modest fruit orchard.

Donna had told her months ago she was retiring from the bakery business this year due to arthritis and to help with her grandkids. Since Tam had thought about expanding, opening a tearoom with pie and pastries seemed like a great idea. She loved tea. Lagrasse locals loved baked goods. Even better, the annual Lagrasse Flavor Festival was just a couple months away—the perfect time to open a new business.

Sitting taller to see the peach trees beyond the fence, Tam turned into Donna's packed dirt driveway. Despite her exchange with the curious man in the bakery yesterday, she prayed Donna would still part with some peaches when the season was in full swing. Jumping out of her green SUV, Tam darted up the sidewalk. She knocked on the screen door of the white clapboard house and waited, breathing in the hypnotizing fragrance of honeysuckle drinking up the morning dew. She twisted around to look for Donna's car, but only saw a small vehicle with a license plate from Florida.

Footfalls approached the other side of the door, and Tam stepped back with a smile. When it opened, she was greeted by Patrick Butler, instead of her business acquaintance.

Light green eyes made a striking contrast against his dark hair and olive complexion, and his cropped, wavy locks lay mussed in a charming way. A giant, well-fed ginger striped cat was curled up in the crook of one of his arms. It looked like it could take down a gazelle. "Oh. Hi, again. I thought… Is Donna here?" she stammered.

"Good morning to you. " His jeans were dusted with white powder and his shirt sleeves rolled up. "Donna already headed over to the bakery. Can I help you?"

Tam flushed with guilt. "Um, no." She couldn't admit she'd come to ask about the peaches behind his back.

The ginger cat yawned lazily, and Tam gaped at the mouth full of sharp teeth. The saber-toothed tiger's owner looked at her in surprise as a second cat, a Siamese kitten, strolled up and rubbed against his ankle. "Nice fur babies," Tam said, trying to figure out how to get peaches and avoid any contact with the cats. "I didn't know Donna had animals."

"They're mine. They're Butlers, too."

"Interesting name." He didn't look like a butler. Her pulse skipped when he leaned one thick shoulder against the door.

"My grandmother was Italian," he replied, unmindful of her curiosity. *"Carbone."*

"Nice heritage. You definitely don't look like an Olsen. She has a son but…"

"Yes, that's Michael. He's…up north."

"I know." Their eyes met in mutual understanding. Michael had left town at seventeen, choosing to live a more transient and experimental lifestyle unless he needed something, and it weighed on Donna like chain mail. Tam tilted her head back and stared at the blooming orchard. She needed to focus on today's tasks, not handsome guests or wayward children. "Do you think you could be talked into reconsidering sharing some of those peaches?"

"I'm sorry," Patrick said, cutting her off with an apologetic tone. He caressed the top of the cat's head like a supervillain.

Tam gawked, and the corner of his mouth twitched. "Is that going to be a problem, Gracious Earth?"

He was teasing her, but she couldn't laugh.

"No," she retorted, then sized him up again. "It may be for Petals and Pie, but I'll think of something."

"Your tearoom?"

"Yes, my daughter named it."

"Well, I'm sure there's room for both of us in Lagrasse."

She gave him a sardonic smile. "Yes, right across the street from each other. Luckily, my business will be new."

"And I sell more than pie. My award-winning pastries will be made fresh every morning."

Tam opened her mouth but no reply came out. Her pies would be purchased from an affordable commercial bakery in Atlanta, and she'd have a few cookies shipped over from Europe. "My teas will be imported and local. And we'll have comfortable seating for people who want to chit-chat or hang out."

"Nice," he said in a flat tone.

The bakery was small and tight with only a small room off to one side. It wasn't exactly a lounging location. Just somewhere to pick up bread. Feeling more confident, Tam motioned toward the fence protecting the peach orchard. "I'm sorry you won't part with any peaches. I thought maybe Donna had planned on it despite what she told you."

"She didn't mention it." Patrick must have

stiffened because the cat in his arm gave her a cold, dead-eyed stare like she'd touched one of its toys.

"I'm sorry if I woke you then," she said, arranging a smile on her face so he couldn't tell she was unnerved. "I better head to the shop."

"I'll tell Donna you stopped by," he replied.

The Siamese kitten on the floor mewed, and Tam glanced at her ankles wondering if she should protect them. "I'm sure I'll see her later. Thanks." She'd head over to The Last Re-Torte as soon as she had a break and get to the bottom of things. Hopefully, he wouldn't be there.

"Have a good morning." Patrick's kitten whined again, and he scooped it up with his free arm. The bigger cat in his embrace made a noise of dissent over his divided attention, and he murmured under his breath in a tone that placated it. Both animals glared at one another, then looked up at him with adoring eyes.

Tam trotted down the steps forcing herself not to look back. It wasn't hard knowing he was buying the bakery that was supposed to shut down. With a frustrated exhale, she climbed into her car. Tapping her teeth to keep from grinding them, she turned over the engine and threw the gearshift into Reverse, but not before glancing at the car parked in front of her. Suddenly, a sneeze that had been brewing exploded from her chest making her hit the brakes. She groaned and reached for a tissue. The handsome but irritatingly cool man had been covered in flour and felines. *No thanks.* In her opinion, cats were nothing but teeth, claws, and toxic dander. She wasn't so sure about Patrick Butler, either.

Minutes later, Tam made the familiar turn onto Loger Street just past the fountain in the center of town to find plenty of parking in front of The Gracious Earth. There was always plenty of parking because the local economy was struggling, especially the small businesses.

Within an hour, she was hungry. She frowned as she unpacked the last of her honey stock from her cousin, Ali Underwood, arranging the jars prettily on a display stand for the local beekeeper. It was hard not to peek across the street and wonder if Donna's replacement had clocked in. Tam hadn't wanted to like the little peach pie as much as she had. Sweet, peachy syrup had flooded through her mouth after she bit through the delicate crust. It'd sent bliss through her veins. Just thinking about it made her mouth water again. No doubt Patrick would refuse to share the recipe.

Her phone had not buzzed. Tam wondered if Donna had received her email. She'd messaged her friend so as not to bother her, and she'd also texted Gretchen about the newcomer across the street this morning.

Tam picked up a container of honey. The gold syrup reminded her of the herb gardens blooming like crazy in her small backyard. Thankfully, honeybees were a well-respected resource in these parts, and her fresh herbs, tinctures, and homemade tea blends for the season would be top-notch—as long as she could get the produce she needed. The herb shop needed more than just popular brands of vitamins and herbal supplements.

The shop door jingled, and Gretchen walked into the store with her youngest child, Emma, in tow. "Gretchen! I was just thinking about the bakery," Tam confessed.

"I got your text," said her fair-haired friend with a grin. Gretchen was almost a mirror image of her mother but with fewer silver streaks in her hair and more prominent curves. Fourteen-month-old Emma toddled over to the pet treats while Gretchen examined the honey products on the shelves. "These look good. New crop?"

"They're from last season, but they're sealed tight."

"I'm sorry I didn't text back. We were on the road." Gretchen motioned toward Emma.

"No problem. I was just wondering if everything was okay at The Last Re-Torte."

"You met Patrick," said Gretchen.

"I did." Tam picked up an empty cardboard box. "He didn't look like a cousin or your brother, but he mentioned ya'll were family friends." Gretchen's smile trembled, and Tam suspected she was thinking of Michael. "I'm sorry. I don't mean to be nosy," Tam blurted. "It's just I went over to see about peaches from your mom's orchard yesterday, and he was there. Then I dropped by the house today, and he was there, too!"

"Yes, Patrick and I have known each other all our lives." Gretchen picked up one of Ali's beeswax lip balms. "I need one of these," she mumbled, and sniffed it. "Mmm."

Tam tried to tamp down her burning questions but failed. "He said he's buying the bakery."

Gretchen capped the tube of beeswax. "That's right. Sorry you keep missing Mom. I'm glad the secret's out. We decided not to say anything until we knew he could get here. The paperwork still has to go through, but he got in touch with Mom about a job here, and everything fell into place." Gretchen gave Tam a half smile. "To be honest, with her rheumatoid arthritis diagnosis, things aren't getting better over there. I just…" Her lips turned down. "It's like I told you before, Tam. I can't take over the bakery. It was always the plan for Michael, but he's not here. I know

Mom wants me to, but I have three children and a husband who need me, and I'm…" She brightened. "I'm expecting."

Tam felt her jaw drop. "You're pregnant?"

"Yes. Again." Gretchen blushed.

Tam threw up her hands with excitement. "Don't say 'again' like that!" Gretchen laughed like she hoped she would. "I'm sorry about your mom, but you are a great mother, and it's a wonderful choice."

A tiny bit of envy tugged on Tam's admiration, but she ignored it. Piper was enough. One child was all she was going to have and there was nothing Tam could do about it. She had her daughter and a shop, and now there was an opportunity for a second business to keep them afloat and help save for college. If she could not have a husband or more children to share her life with, she would give her all to Piper and cultivate the good earth's issue. "I'm happy for you," she assured her friend. "Four is a good number."

"Thanks. And Patrick is a great guy. He was on his own in Miami." She glanced through the front window toward the bakery. "Until he got custody of the kids."

"You mean there's more than one?"

Gretchen laughed. "Yes, Scarlet and the baby. He just adopted Jax."

"Oh, yes, I saw him yesterday. The baby's adorable, but the man has his hands full."

"He does. Jax is eight months, and Scarlet is twelve."

"Then Piper should know her," replied Tam in astonishment. "She's twelve, too. Where's their mother?" she wondered. She turned to the shelf, a blush warming her cheeks. Why did she want to know? It wasn't her business. His repertoire of baked goods was what mattered, especially pie. Luckily, Gretchen seemed nonplussed.

"Scarlet's mother had custody but rarely let Patrick see her. He let it go since he didn't want to traumatize Scarlet with court battles, and he worked crazy hours anyway. Then some awful things came to light, and both children were removed from their mother. Patrick got legal custody almost right away even though Jax isn't his child."

"He said he worked in restaurants. Can he handle a whole bakery as a single father?"

Gretchen smiled. "Yes. I'm sure of it. He started in the food industry after culinary school and worked his way up to five-star establishments. His ex accepted child support but made visitation nearly impossible."

"That's sad," mused Tam.

"It was." Gretchen looked across the street. "He used to visit us every summer with his parents until he graduated high school, but now he wants to settle in Lagrasse for good. The problem is he needs to get something going with two children to care for, or he'll have to go back to Florida and take a job he turned down."

"Poor guy," Tam murmured.

"Yes, it was a Michelin starred restaurant—one of the most famous in the South and an incredible job opportunity. But he wanted to get Scarlet out of Miami and give her real roots."

Patrick Butler had given up a prestigious opportunity to move to a new hometown and raise children on his own? Tam softened with admiration for the selfless act until she remembered the peaches. "By the way, I'm going to need peaches. Do you think your mom will have any extra?"

Gretchen shook her head. "Last year's are gone. She offered what's ripening now to Patrick."

"So I heard. I just wanted to make sure." Tam looked at her empty canister of *Peaceful Peach*. There were only a few lavender flakes left in the bottom. "I guess I'll have to either wait or run over to Brook's Grocery and buy a few pounds that aren't local and fresh."

"I'm sorry," said Gretchen earnestly. "Mom's hoping he'll take over the orchard, too, so she doesn't have to worry about that anymore. It's just become too much for us with Michael gone."

"I understand," said Tam. "I wish I would have gotten to her first, though." Tam glanced at the wall dividing her store from the empty space next door that would become Petals and Pie. "Maybe someday I can grow my own, but first I have to get the new business up and running."

"If anyone can do it, you can." Gretchen held up the lip balm. "I told Patrick I'd fill in for a half hour so he could pick up Scarlet from school. They needed 'bonding' time. Ring this lip balm up for me?"

Minutes later, Tam watched her friend traipse across the street to the bakery. It was clear she would not be getting her peaches from Donna this year, and worse, The Last Re-Torte wasn't closing. Would Petals and Pie be successful with a bakery just across the street? She exhaled. She needed a winner, not just something to get by.

Her stomach rumbled again, making her nerves twinge. The real questions were, could a man with two children run a bakery on his own, and why was she craving another peach pie so badly?

Chapter Two

The single-story, beige-and-brown middle school looked about as exciting as a warehouse. Patrick cringed as he moved up in the pickup line on Wednesday, wondering about the first words out of Scarlet's mouth if she spoke to him at all. He tried not to let his fatigue make him grumpy. Donna and he'd had a long night discussing how to phase out her hours once he signed the papers on the bakery. He'd have to hire employees, eventually, and get an accountant soon, too. Bookkeeping was not his favorite. It was a tall order with the upgrades the business needed and the state of his children. Scarlet, in particular.

Preteens dressed in tees and polo shirts crowded the long perpendicular sidewalk in front of the school; a few brave souls wore shorts with cowboy or hiking boots. He scanned the students, looking for Scarlet's straight dark hair. When he spied a hoodie, he paused, then exhaled. Of course his daughter was wearing a long-sleeved top on a sunny, warm day. He groaned but reminded himself it could have been worse. At least it was thin.

Just like the day before, Scarlet made no effort to watch for him as he rolled along, and when Patrick was near enough for her to hear him, he gave the horn a sharp beep. She didn't look up. She had her back to her peers and was facing the building with a book in her hand instead of a tablet. But to be fair, he'd cut off her Wi-Fi and social media access until they could get settled and find a new therapist—another reason she detested him. He waited with a clenched stomach, watching the driver behind him tap the steering wheel. It was tempting to roll the window down and call out, but she'd be mortified.

Patrick waited another eternal minute, then, with a sigh, moved along, searching for a parking spot in the teachers' lot. A glimpse into the back showed Jax had fallen asleep in his car seat, and Patrick grumbled under his breath. He'd have to wake up Jax and carry the baby while he fetched Scarlet, but Jax hardly blinked when Patrick lofted him over his shoulder and strode across the lot. Nodding at a teacher on traffic duty, he wove through the thinning crowd of kids and stopped a few feet away from Scarlet. Her head had dropped lower as if concentrating on every word, but he suspected she was pretending. He took a breath, heart prickling with concern that he might startle her. "Scarlet?"

She jerked her head, hazel eyes almost black. "What?" She sounded as if she knew he'd been standing there all along.

Patrick felt as if someone had jerked his reins. "I sat over there in the car for five minutes." He pointed at the pickup line. "Come on. I'm parked in the teachers' lot now."

Scarlet gave him a piercing stare, and he bit down on his frustration. "I need to get Jax home," he said, instead of telling her to hurry. He started back for the car, but not before noticing how her eyes darted around looking for spectators. After a few seconds of not hearing her following him, Patrick peeked and saw she was taking her time getting her things together. Exasperated, he stopped at the end of the sidewalk to wait instead of starting across the parking lot without her. "Ready?" he called. She trudged toward him, looking at the ground. He noticed a few kids watching and wondered if she could feel their gazes. Just then, a green SUV zipped alongside the curb in front of him, and he jumped backward as a girl darted past him to climb inside.

"Sorry!" she called in a friendly tone. He nodded as she swung open the door, then he caught a glimpse of her chauffeur and froze. Tam Rochester leaned toward him, brows lowered to her lashes. "Hey. Gretchen told me you had a daughter here."

Scarlet's footsteps came up behind him. Her silence was deafening as she listened to every word. Despite the tension, he smiled at the savvy entrepreneur. "I'm picking her up." He put an arm on Scarlet's shoulder and nudged her forward. She jerked out of his reach.

Tam said nothing about the girl's reaction to his touch. "Hi, there. Nice hoodie." She smiled at Scarlet until the girl gave a small nod. "I talked to your Aunt Gretchen yesterday," she added cheerfully. "She told me you'd be going to school here."

A pause hung in the air before Scarlet spoke. "She's not my real aunt."

"She's like an aunt," Patrick supplied, mortified at her disrespectful tone.

Tam was oblivious, or pretended to be. She motioned at the girl beside her, who looked like a miniature version of herself, only blonde. "You're right. I'm sorry. This is my daughter, Piper. She's in seventh grade."

"So is Scarlet," said Patrick, trying to sound like this was amazing news.

Tam caught the hint, and so did Piper. She examined Scarlet, unblinking. "Saw you in the science lab."

"Yeah," said Scarlet after an awkward pause. She shifted on her feet, then pulled her hood down, letting her dark hair shine in the sun.

Tam gave Patrick a small smile. "Maybe you two girls could study for tests together," she suggested. "Piper is class president."

Scarlet gave a soft snort. "I don't need to study. They're not going to make me take them since I just got here."

"Okay." Piper shrugged, nonplussed, then they all waited, the air between them growing stale.

Patrick's frantic mind tried to settle on something else to say.

Tam rescued him from the mental panic. "We better get on toward home. Nice to see you again."

"You, too," said Patrick. And he meant it. Despite her disappointment that he was buying the bakery, she'd been nice to Scarlet. He shifted Jax onto his other shoulder. "Did you find any peaches?"

Her smile rippled. "Not yet," she answered in a cool tone. "It was nice to meet you, Scarlet. I hope we see you again."

Scarlet remained silent. Tam gave them both a wave, and Patrick waved back. He was suddenly flooded with regret that he'd refused to part with any peaches. It was silly. He could find a way. "There," he said, as Scarlet walked beside him back to the car. "She seems nice—Piper. How were your other classes?" His daughter remained mute. After they climbed in, Patrick let the radio do the talking for the first few minutes, then tried again. "How'd the bus ride go this morning?"

"Lame."

"How were your other classes besides Science?"

"Are you going to interrogate me all night?" Scarlet blurted.

Patrick didn't miss a beat. He could take the heat in a kitchen. "No, just until we get home."

"You mean to Ms. Donna's house."

"It's home for now. Better than a hot, roach-infested apartment, isn't it?"

"Mom did the best she could," Scarlet shot back.

Patrick murmured, "I didn't mean it like that. I just meant you have more room to walk and play."

She groaned. "Play? I'm almost thirteen."

Patrick's heart drooped. Scarlet had been cook, housekeeper, and caretaker for a fatherless newborn—and her mother—while she was under the influence or partying. The young girl had been overly relied upon when staying with her handicapped maternal grandparents in the swampy countryside, too. "You're never too old to play. Maybe you can do something with Piper sometime."

"I just met her," mumbled Scarlet. "She's not my type."

"I'm sure there're lots of other nice kids here."

Scarlet gave Patrick a disgusted squint, then turned to the window. After a long pause, he said, "Jax did well today. I think we're going to be able to make this work."

"It'd be better if you let me stay home and take care of him."

"You have school."

"I can homeschool."

"You don't have to watch him all the time, Scarlet. It's my responsibility. You enjoy school while you can before summer gets here."

She exhaled loudly. "What's to enjoy? It's lame."

"It's a nice town. There's a lake. Atlanta's just an hour or so away." Patrick thought of Tam. Her daughter seemed okay.

"Lagrasse is microscopic, and there's no palm trees. It's nothing like home," Scarlet complained.

"Change can be good, and different can be nice. Just give it time."

She fell into silence. Patrick simmered with exasperation. "Who'd you sit with at lunch?"

For some reason, this pressed her last button.

"Please leave me alone. I don't want to answer any more questions!" Scarlet choked on a sob, and stunned, Patrick clamped his jaws shut.

Fine. She was grieving—for the life she'd lost and the life she'd never had. Her mother's lack of care and eventual prison sentence for drug dealing had left gaping canyons inside her that might never fill in—at least not for a long time. But none of this was Scarlet's fault. Patrick hoped Lagrasse would soften the pain. He prayed he could convince her that she was worthy of love with no strings attached and give her a home to heal her heart.

Thursday morning, Ali breezed through the door of The Gracious Earth with almost three-year-old, Alice, at her heels. The sight of her cousin buoyed Tam's spirits, which sagged under the weight of to-do lists. "Hey, cousin!" Tam called as she hurried to help Ali with the boxes she was juggling. One was much lighter than the glass jars filled with honey the beekeeper usually brought in. "What's this?"

"A new idea," grinned Ali.

"Well, you have my attention."

"I brought more honeycomb and lip balm, but I wanted you to try something."

They carried the boxes over to the counter, and Tam peeked. A plastic bag full of curious-looking powder sat inside. "What are you up to now?"

"I wanted to see how well dehydrated honey would go over here in the shop."

Tam picked up a small bag with interest. It looked like it was full of golden sugar granules. "How did you do this?"

"It's not as hard as you think. Since you've been dehydrating fruits and flowers for your new line of herbal teas, I thought I'd give it a whirl, too, but with honey."

Tam held up the dehydrated honey and studied it. "How long does it last?"

"Indefinitely, if you keep the moisture out."

"That's brilliant," Tam exclaimed. She thought of her tearoom. "How are you going to package it? Single servings would be great for Petals and Pie."

"That's the idea," agreed Ali. "Makes less mess, too." The petite redhead looked over her shoulder to check on her daughter, who was toddling around the shop touching things. Tam set down the dried honey and held out her arms to Alice. "How's my sweet baby girl?"

Alice hurried over for a hug. Tam picked her up and rocked her back and forth until she giggled and squirmed down.

Ali sighed. "She's into doing everything by herself now. I had to put a deadbolt on the back-door to make sure she doesn't get outside by her-self, since she's mastered childproof handles."

"That's smart of you. Can't be too careful at this age." Tam glanced across the street through the window, and Ali followed her gaze.

"Have you seen Mystery Man again?"

"You mean Mr. Mom?" Tam flushed, wish-ing she would have shown a little more restraint while chatting with Ali about Lagrasse's newest citizen over the phone. "No. Not since Tuesday, other than waving at each other from across the road."

"How many kids does he have again?"

"So far I've counted a baby, a teenager, and two cats."

"And he's hoarding Donna's peaches."

"Yes," grumbled Tam. "Not that I blame him. His little handheld peach pies are divine."

"I'm going to need to judge for myself," joked Ali. "They'll make or break my support. Will he still bake bread?"

"He didn't go into detail other than to inform me he's a pastry chef. I just know he's here, has baggage, and the bakery is staying open." Tam took a flustered breath.

"So?" Ali grinned at her with mischief. "In-vite him over for tea. Maybe he'll be a little more willing to share and discuss his recipes."

"You know I don't have time to bake. I'm

using the commercial bakery in Atlanta to save money, and he's already interfered with my peach order." Tam frowned. Ordering from the bakery across the street wouldn't make sense. She'd have to mark up, and why would anyone buy a treat from her when they could buy the same thing across the street for less?

"There's enough business in town for everybody, Tam," Ali assured her. "Your teas are doing well in the herb shop, and people are spreading the word that a tearoom will be opening soon."

"I know I shouldn't panic," agreed Tam. "But a second business on my own and now this?"

"You're going to get there," Ali assured her. "You always do."

Tam tried to smile. "Thanks."

"No, Alice!" Ever on the alert, Ali raced across the room to keep the little girl from toppling a tea dispenser as she tried to remove the chrome cover. Alice whimpered.

"They are pretty, aren't they?" Tam soothed her. "They'll be moved over to the tearoom eventually." She walked over and scooped out a few colorful petals for the little girl to hold in her hand. Alice beamed with gratitude.

"Thank you, Tam. You're so thoughtful." Ali sighed. "Don't worry about the bakery. It's never been an issue, and tea and pie is an amazing idea. I'm sure you'll find a way to coexist."

Tam nodded weakly.

Ali pulled out her cell phone and checked the time. "Oops, I need to pick up the twins for Kylee Hollister. She's staying after school today for a parent-teacher meeting."

Ali often babysat Kylee's two sets of twins. "How's the babysitting going?" Tam managed to ask as her mind swirled over the future.

"It's okay, but I don't see Henry and Annabelle as much since they started first grade." Ali gave a sad smile. "I do have to admit their twin baby brother and sister are easier, and Alice likes having friends nearer her age."

"You could get her a puppy," mumbled Tam, wondering how any parents on earth could manage two sets of twins like the Hollisters did. "Piper and I are getting a dog…someday, when things slow down." And when Piper went away to school, Tam would at least have company.

"Trooper is quite enough, thanks," Ali laughed, referring to her family's border collie. She reached for Alice's hand. "Tell Tam goodbye, honey bug."

The little girl waggled her fingers as the door chimes rattled. A couple in matching T-shirts stamped with *The Peach State* wandered inside. Tam shifted her attention to her customers as Ali slipped out. After greeting them, she moved Ali's new honey stock from the counter to the floor to look busy. When she finished, she saw the woman standing in front of the herbal tea dispensers reading the labels. Tam hurried over. "Thanks for coming in today. Are you looking for something particular?"

From across the room by the honey jars, the husband joked, "She's always looking, and she's very particular."

Tam chuckled as his wife rolled her eyes and pointed at the canister of Strawberry Strut. "That sounds nice. What brand is it?"

"The loose leaf teas are my own recipes," Tam informed her with pride. "The chamomile is home grown. Strawberry Strut has local strawberries, lime peel and basil with just a hint of walnut. The walnut is home-grown, too." The woman scooted closer to the empty container of Peaceful Peach. "I'm allergic to nuts. Do you have any more of that?"

Tam winced. "No, I'm sorry. I wish I did. I use local ingredients, and my peach supply is out."

"That's too bad," said the lady.

"Hey, Ruby!" called her husband. Tam had hoped there would be a honey purchase, too, but the gentleman was standing in front of the window looking across the street. "Look at the sign at the bakery over there. They have little peach pies!"

"That's where the smell was coming from," said Ruby. "We're going to have to check it out."

She sent Tam a fleeting grin. "I wish you had more of the peach tea. I'd love to try it."

"Let me get you a business card," Tam suggested. Ruby nodded, and Tam hurried to the register for her stack.

"We're just passing through town, but thank you for showing me around," Ruby said. "It's nice you have vitamins, herbs, and locally grown products here."

"You'll have to come back," Tam invited her. "We'll be opening a tearoom next door soon."

"I will." Ruby held out her hand for the card, then waved goodbye.

Tam watched the couple hurry across the street, all thoughts of teas and honey evaporating after spotting the neatly printed sign in the window of The Last Re-Torte announcing handheld treats. She'd just lost two customers to Patrick Butler's peach pies.

Chapter Three

After rearranging jars of peaches on the pantry shelf, Patrick roused Jax from his nap and met Donna at the register. "I thought you had an appointment," he said with a confused frown.

She smiled. "I rescheduled it. I thought I'd come in and look over the books while you got Scarlet."

"Do you want me to come back to close up?"

Donna waved Patrick off. "No, no problem. There'll be just a half hour left until closing. You taking over the baking has taken a huge load off of me." She pointed at the big bag on the counter. "Did someone forget their purchase?"

Patrick felt his cheeks warm. "We had a couple customers walk over from Tam's herb shop today. I think she recommended us, and I wanted to thank her."

"Oh, what a sweetheart. She always does that during spring break and the Flavor Festival."

Patrick wrinkled his forehead. "What's a flavor festival?"

"It's a local event to draw people into town. We have it at the beginning of the summer, and it's a great business booster. We really need it this year."

"Sounds interesting." Patrick motioned at the bag. "I thought I'd give Tam a couple jars of last year's peaches although I'm using them for hand pies."

"The pies are selling like hotcakes," Donna marveled.

"It just makes sense for people who don't want a whole pie."

"You're right," agreed Donna. "I tried selling pie by the slice, but it didn't go over like I hoped. You're a genius. Hand pies are perfect."

"Thanks." Patrick jostled Jax on his hip. He wondered if he should mention that to Tam. The baby gurgled at Donna, and she cooed back. "Well, I'll just drop this off on my way to the school," said Patrick.

Donna winked. "It's nice of you. Between the shop and her daughter, Tam's always on the go, so I know she'll appreciate it."

He shrugged like it was nothing. "How was Scarlet this morning? Did she get on the bus okay?"

"She did, grudgingly, but she wasn't rude. I think she likes me."

"Then you're making progress. Thanks for doing that."

"Give her time," Donna chided him. "It's hard being a girl at this age, and she's coming out of a bad situation."

Remorse jabbed Patrick in the chest. "I know. I just can't believe I wasn't aware of what was going on." He looked around the bakery. "If and when I have things together, I'll see about a place to live and get us out of your hair."

Donna shooed him away. "Don't you worry about that right now."

He smiled meekly. "I just want to fix everything—prove to her that I'm more than she believes I am and help her understand right and wrong."

"In time."

"You're right," Patrick sighed. "It's hard. Especially doing this on my own."

Donna inclined her head. "Someday Scarlet will thank you for this—and her mother, too. And you *will* find the person who belongs at your side—someone who will love the kids as much as you do. Don't give up."

Patrick wanted to tell her that after twelve years he had little reason to have faith in the idea. He'd been devastated when his ex-wife asked for a divorce, and he'd kept too busy for any more heartbreak since. He'd filled the holes in his heart with baking, and with Jax and Scarlet now a full-time responsibility, he saw little reason to risk another romantic relationship. Besides, where would he find someone in little Lagrasse?

Jax hooted and reached for the bag, and Patrick remembered his mission. "I'll see you in a bit," he promised, "and I'll make dinner tonight."

"You're a wonderful boy," Donna called after him.

He chuckled as he hurried out with Jax to fetch Scarlet, then remembered that he still had the bag for Tam. As he started across the street, the door to The Gracious Earth opened, and she flipped a sign over and locked the door behind her. When she started for her SUV, Patrick looked both ways and crossed over to meet her. The afternoon sunshine felt heavy, but velvety petunias blooming in cement planters on her side of the street danced in a breeze. "Hey," he called as she reached for the driver's side door. Jax shrieked in delight as he bounced along in Patrick's arms.

Tam turned in surprise, and a smile on her face dissolved. He held out the bag. "I just wanted to thank you for sending those customers over today."

Her blue eyes clouded, but she let him place

the bag into her arms. "Thanks." She looked startled at the weight. "What's this?"

"Canned peaches. And thank you for saying hi to Scarlet yesterday," Patrick added. "I'm praying she'll settle in soon and meet people."

"Well, Piper knows who she is now." Tam's tone sounded more stiff than polite.

"That's great. She doesn't have any friends," Patrick began.

"It's a small town. I'm sure she will soon," interjected Tam.

"I mean she's never really been able to before because…" Patrick stopped himself. Tam looked tense. "She's just had a lot of responsibility. Her mom… She's in a correctional facility and will be for a long time." Patrick's chest tightened as an awkward silence grew between them.

Jax babbled something that sounded like *bye*. It turned into a sneeze, and he giggled. Tam's expression softened. "Gretchen told me a little bit. It's good of you to take in the kids." She held up the bag. "Thanks for the peaches, I guess."

"You guess?" he teased. He couldn't help himself. Her bristly demeanor today begged for a little teasing. Her hair looked silky and her freckles lively and cute. But something in her eyes was missing.

"It would have been better if I could have gotten a fresh bushel to dehydrate," she admitted. "Canned peaches are different, but they'll work."

Patrick pictured the rows of peach trees in Donna's orchard. "Maybe I can spare a few," he began halfheartedly, but she held up a hand to stop him.

"I've already made do. I contacted an orchard owner near Albany."

"I'm sorry about the change."

"It is what it is." Tam unrolled the bag, looked inside, then eyeballed him. "I assume you don't share your recipes, either."

He smiled. "Never."

"Of course not."

"What about your teas?" Patrick replied, suspecting he might be poking a bear. "I'd love to try my hand. The bakery could use some new beverage choices."

Tam's jaw dropped. "What?"

"Let me guess. Your tea formulas aren't for sale."

"Of course they're not," Tam exclaimed. "I'm trying to send my daughter to college in five years."

Patrick studied her just as Jax tittered and made her surrender a dazzling smile. She reached for the baby's hand, and he wrapped his fist around her index finger. Her sky-blue eyes were hypnotizing. Something bloomed in

Patrick's chest like a flower opening to the sun. He wanted her to understand. "I thought I was just coming to work here at first, to find a home for my children, but Donna has found out her aches and pains were more serious. She needs me, and I need the bakery to succeed for my children. They need a safe, permanent home."

Tam's gaze flickered with something like concern. "I get it. And I wish you luck," she said with a heavy exhale.

"Thanks. I think."

She pointed toward The Gracious Earth and the empty real estate beside it. "Do you see that space there? I've wanted to sell my own teas for years, and Petals and Pie is the perfect way. It's going to be a meeting place— the heart of the town, I hope. It'd make my daughter and me more comfortable, that's for sure, and now's the time since the photography studio there closed."

"Times are tough for everybody." Patrick's chest tangled with emotions. A tea and pie room across from a bakery. Surely most people would want to sit down with a cup of tea and relax while they ate rather than dash in and out of an old bakery. He would have to do more than repaint. He'd need it to be irresistible. Patrick realized Tam could see the calculations in his eyes and cleared his throat. "I better head over to the school and get Scarlet," he mumbled.

"I'm right behind you," she echoed in a companionable tone as she climbed into her car.

Yes, yes you are.

But he couldn't help but like the sound of her singsong voice. He almost stumbled on his way back to where he'd parked as his mind roved in circles. He was no stranger to competition in the pastry business, but he didn't know what to do about the woman across the street. She wasn't just throwing a wrench into his plans with her intentions, she was stirring up feelings of interest he had no time to deal with right now.

Chapter Four

The ride to school on Monday morning was cheerful as Piper shared her excitement for the end of the year. "I'm proud of you," said Tam. "Making honor roll every reporting period is a huge accomplishment."

"Thanks, Mom. I know I can do it again if I do well on my last Social Studies test."

"You will," Tam assured her. She squinted in the bright morning sunshine as they traveled down the smooth country road toward the school. "Now I may be late picking you up," she warned Piper, as her mind went over her schedule. Her stomach tightened. It was impossible not to think about her appointment with the bank that morning. To sign the papers for the second lease was huge, especially before the Flavor Festival. She'd have to start cleaning out the space as soon as she had the documentation in order. She needed to hire cleaners and painters, round up tables and decor, refurbish the small kitchen in the back, order supplies, and of course, stock up her tea line.

Her throat ran dry. It was a big risk, but she'd taken the leap before with The Gracious Earth. She'd become an entrepreneur all on her own after her ex had left her and Piper with nothing. There was no reason she couldn't do it again. The bakery across the street might offer a little competition, but she'd have to make the best of it. Her stomach pinched against the pressure. It was hard to be antagonistic toward the man she'd seen slink into church with his children and Donna yesterday, especially since—

"Mom?"

"What?"

"Turn."

"Oh!" Tam chuckled and did a U-turn after missing the entrance to the school.

"Nervous about the bank?" guessed Piper.

"Yes, but I'm fine. It just seems crazy carrying two leases, but we need the room if we're going to throw tea parties." Tam gave her daughter a grin.

Piper smiled back. "It'll be fun. My friends are excited."

"Good." Tam relaxed. Piper might not have a traditional family and all of the things the other girls in town did, but she had a steady and loving relationship with her mom. That was something.

Tam thought about Patrick's moody daughter and felt bad for him. "Wish me luck."

"Break a leg."

"I hope not. And Piper," Tam added, "don't forget to be nice to Scarlet today. She's having a tough time."

Piper's brows raised with exaggerated doubt. "Okay. I'll try."

"Just—" Tam waggled her eyebrows "—lay on the Piper Sniper charm."

Piper laughed as she escaped the car. Tam drove back to Lagrasse, trundled over the railroad tracks past Brook's Grocery, and climbed the small incline into downtown and its central park, where an old historical fountain gurgled. She turned left at the firehouse, then circled around to the bank two doors down, just as the parking lot was coming to life with minivans and pickup trucks. Sign the papers. Get to work. A second store could mean a better life and future for her baby girl if God answered their prayers.

By the end of the week, Patrick thought the small of his back would pop after carrying Jax to keep him content for so many hours. He almost cried when Donna arrived and took over. She praised his warm peach and strawberry pies, took him to task for altering her oatmeal cookie recipe, then started a round of sourdough bread before he lugged himself to the back office to change Jax's diaper and feed him lunch. Afterward, rather than pass out for a nap like he wanted, he put the baby in a small umbrella stroller Gretchen had found for him and went for a walk.

Springtime was lighter in Lagrasse than the summers he remembered, and the humidity was milder than his former tropical climate. Warm sunshine mixed with cool air. It was scented with fragrances he tried to recognize as his brain scrambled to recall what grew in the middle of Georgia—azaleas, early roses, hearty petunias, and pansies—all of them painting the landscape with vivid colors against the pines and azure skies. Jax bounced his legs with enthusiasm, and Patrick smiled to himself as he cruised up the block examining other businesses—a butcher shop, antiques, lawyer's office, dental care, upscale clothing consignment store, and then the town square that was a green space with a playground and fountain. He sat on a bench and let Jax watch the beautiful Victorian era fountain for a while, then took the baby out and bounced him on a slide at the small playground as children darted around them with squeals of happiness. A little girl with pigtails flew by, and his heart fluttered. It could have been Scarlet, but she'd had few moments like this. And he'd missed out because he hadn't wanted to rock the boat. He'd been dead wrong. He should have insisted on sharing custody despite the challenges of co-parenting and legal issues. At least she would have known he cared.

He exhaled, heavy regret still taking residence in his lungs no matter how he tried to get a grip on things. Jax looked up at him with a toothy grin. Smiling, Patrick picked him up and tossed him into the air.

"Careful, there." He turned in surprise at Gretchen's greeting. She grinned at him, Emma on her hip. "This is my friend, Ali Underwood, and her daughter, Alice." She pointed at a petite redhead beside her. "I see you escaped the kitchen."

"Yes, your mom's there." He nodded at Ali, who was trying to keep hold of the hand of a little girl. "It's nice to meet you."

"You, too. I've heard a lot about you."

"Oh?" Patrick wondered from whom.

Ali shot a glance at Gretchen, the side of her mouth curling up. "Not from me," Gretchen protested. "Ali is Tam's cousin and also our local beekeeper. Her husband, Heath, is an accountant and math professor. He's great, by the way."

So word had gotten around. Patrick wondered what Tam had told her cousin. He'd seen her from across the street and always made an effort to wave. That included the car pickup line the day before, too. "Do you sell honey? I use it sometimes as a sweetener alternative."

"I do," admitted the vibrant woman. She grinned. "I'm Tam's supplier."

He raised his chin in acknowledgment. "Then I shouldn't intervene."

"Intervene? You're more than welcome to purchase it. I sell to Donna."

"Harding Honey," Gretchen prodded him.

"That's right," he said, remembering a jar on Donna's kitchen counter.

"Harding was my name before I married my second husband," Ali explained. She motioned toward Alice as if she was an asset, as well.

"How do you do it?" Patrick motioned toward the tugging toddler. "Run a business and care for a child?"

"Teamwork. My husband and I have two. We make it happen."

"Teamwork," agreed Patrick. He'd worked in kitchens long enough to understand that, but he didn't have a team. Not even a partner.

Gretchen smiled. "I'm glad you're here. Mom's already calmer. She isn't acting like this is the end of the world, and I can get things done."

"You haven't spoken to her since I added cranberries to the oatmeal cookies."

"Uh-oh." Gretchen hummed in low warning. "That's sacrilegious."

He grinned. "We'll see if they sell."

"They sound good to me," said Ali with enthusiasm.

Gretchen let a doubtful smile pinch her cheeks. Jax jabbered again, then put his fingers in his mouth. A violent sneeze followed. "I better get this boy back for a nap," Patrick decided. "And make sure he's not getting a cold."

"It could be allergies," Ali pointed out. He raised his brows. It'd never occurred to him. Should he take Jax to a doctor? He'd scheduled a routine checkup to meet a pediatrician, but it was six weeks away. "I'll see about that." Great. Another worry.

After a friendly goodbye, Patrick strapped Jax into his stroller again, caressing the apple of his cheek before lugging the buggy back onto the sidewalk to cross the square to the other side of Loger Street. After passing different storefronts, including a realty office where he picked up a free listings magazine, he stopped in front of a long, empty window that ended at a craftsman style wood door painted dark blue. Lettering had peeled off the glass window beside it. He stepped back. Leonard Photography, it had once read. The photography store. He peered inside. The square footage was a big, empty room. Hardwood floors. White walls. There was a counter at the back beside a hall that led to what he surmised was a studio or dressing rooms. It looked stark. Plain. Industrial.

Jax sneezed loudly again.

"Is everything okay?"

Patrick twitched in surprise. Tam stood a few feet away, having just let herself out of The Gracious Earth next door. She held a small coil of wire with two dangling brass keys. There was a tablet under her arm.

"Hey," he replied, trying not to flush because she'd caught him examining her new space.

"Hi." Jax whooped a delighted sound of recognition. She didn't bat an eye. "Hi, baby," she said, barely looking down.

"I was just checking the place out. The For Lease sign is gone."

"Yes, I signed everything on Monday."

"There's nothing like a nice cup of tea," Patrick blustered. "I'm sure you'll do very well."

"Do you think so?"

"I didn't mean that just because I sell pies, too. It'll be fine." He hoped.

She twiddled the keys around her finger. "Well, as my cousin Ali says, 'There's room enough in Lagrasse for everybody.'"

"So she agrees with me." He grinned.

Tam fought a chuckle. "I'm afraid I'm just a little bullheaded when it comes to business."

"It's only natural with your daughter getting older."

Tam smiled faintly. "I'm glad you understand."

"I understand needing to prepare for the future."

Jax sneezed again. She crouched down and studied him, then looked up at Patrick. "Have you considered this little one might have allergies?"

He nodded. "Your cousin just suggested that a few minutes ago."

"After he's a year old, you can start giving him honey," Tam informed Patrick. "Local honey is great for that."

"Thanks. I'll check into it. What about for now?"

"Talk to your doctor first," said Tam, rising to her feet. "He's such a darling baby." She wore cornflower blue fitted slacks that accentuated her trim waist. A matching pin-striped blouse made her azure eyes blaze, and the blue against her cheeks made her look sweet. Patrick slammed on the mental brakes in his head.

"I used organic berries and cold compresses for Piper when she was small," Tam continued, oblivious to the feathers of attraction that had just fluttered over him. "I have some natural nasal sprays and eye drops for little ones next door if you decide to go that route. Just try to keep him inside when he gets like this. The pollen will settle down in a few weeks."

"Thanks," stammered Patrick, trying to refocus. "I should get him back over to the bakery to lie down for a bit. Donna has to pick up one of the grands from school today."

Tam gave him a nod. "I need to get inside here and measure the space. I plan to have the grand opening during the Flavor Festival."

"The festival," Patrick repeated. His chest tingled. The festival would be the perfect time for a grand reopening. She wouldn't like it.

"You look disappointed."

"I was just thinking a grand reopening that week would be a good idea," Patrick admitted. "Actually, it's been in the back of my mind for a while."

Tam's thick, short lashes blinked, and the corners of her smile disappeared. They stared at each other for a few seconds until she forced her gaze away. "Well, I guess we'll both be celebrating."

Patrick tried to look enthusiastic. "It could be fun."

"All the pie we can eat," she mumbled.

He forced a smile. "Well, I need to think about it and make sure I could even be ready. But good luck. I better get back to work. Baking to do and all that."

"See you later." Tam nodded. "Take care of Jax."

"I will." Patrick gave her what he hoped was a friendly wave. She was sweet to be concerned about the baby, although he could tell she wasn't pleased he wanted to do a grand reopening at the same time she opened her tearoom. It wasn't that big a deal, he hoped. Like she'd pointed out, there was room for both of them in Lagrasse. And he planned to stay.

Tam craned her neck to see over the crowd of students until she spotted Piper with her usual circle of friends. Her daughter didn't seem to mind that Tam was a few minutes late due to daydreaming in the tearoom. Spotting her, Piper waved to her friends, then dashed over to the car, swung open the door, and hopped inside.

"Good Monday?"

"Great day," exclaimed Piper. "I got an A on my Social Studies test last Friday."

"That's excellent. I'm proud of you."

Piper smiled. "I can't wait to be in high school."

Tam groaned. "I know. One more year."

"Right. And I can work at the tearoom after school. I'll be fourteen."

Tam eased through the car pickup line. "I'm sure we can work something out." She was pleased Piper wanted to help pay her way even though she'd move off. Hopefully, she wouldn't want to spread her wings too far. Tam's brother had gone to Arizona. She'd moved only as far as Lagrasse from Columbus, Georgia, and her parents had packed up from there and moved to Florida.

"Oh, look," said Piper. She pointed to the end of the schoolyard. Dressed in her thin hoodie, Scarlet sat on the curb with her chin in her hands. Tam glanced at the rearview mirror. There was only a woman in a minivan behind her picking up a pair of rambunctious boys in baseball jerseys.

"It looks like her dad's not here yet," Tam mused. She glanced at the clock. "Sorry I was late."

Piper shrugged. "That's okay. I knew you'd be here."

Something pricked Tam's heart, suggesting perhaps Scarlet didn't have the same confidence in her father. Being late was something Patrick should try to avoid right now. She eased to a stop beside the girl, and Piper lowered the window. Scarlet stared.

"Do you need a ride?" Tam called.

Scarlet's cheeks reddened. "I'm waiting on my father."

"We can take you home," Tam offered. She wondered if the bakery was busy. Why would he put off picking up his daughter otherwise?

Scarlet shook her head. "It's fine."

Piper looked over at Tam, hesitant. Teachers had returned inside. Most of the cars had diminished. "I think I'm going to make an executive decision," Tam announced.

Scarlet climbed to her feet, holding a thick notebook to her chest. "I'm okay."

"Just in case, hop into the back seat and come home with Piper and me. We can give your dad a call." The sun blazed down on Scarlet's dark hair and unsure expression. She had to be roasting. "We have ice cream." Tam winked. A lecture was taking shape in her mind for Patrick. Piper had to grow up with a disinterested, absent father. It wasn't fair for Scarlet to do the same when hers had custody.

"We do," said Piper on cue. "Brownie Chocolate Chip. You should come."

Scarlet looked uneasy, but Tam hit the lock on the door. "Jump in." The girl climbed into the back after a long pause. "Here." Tam handed back her cell phone. "Shoot him a text and let him know you'll be at our house."

Piper twisted around in her seat. "I can give

you our address." The girls talked as Tam pulled out onto the highway. She reached for the radio to turn it up but stopped, her hand in midair as Piper emitted a giggle and to her surprise, Scarlet snickered. Yes, the food fight in the cafeteria had been hilarious—but only because they weren't a part of it and didn't get into trouble.

Tam grinned, listening as Scarlet's guarded responses became friendlier after she passed Tam's phone back up front. By the time they pulled into the driveway, the girls were comparing notes on a new young adult film based on their favorite book and talking about an actor Tam didn't know. She dished out ice cream as both girls collapsed onto the couch.

"Scarlet, you can take off your hoodie if you want. We don't keep it that cold in here," she teased from the kitchen door.

The girl made a noise of amusement, then slid out of the top.

"Oh, I like your shirt," said Piper.

Tam glanced across the room and set the ice cream scooper down in surprise. "Gloria Estefan?"

"Vintage," said Piper.

Tam stuck out her tongue. "Yes, I know. I grew up in the nineties. I am vintage."

The girls laughed. Even Scarlet. "Did you listen to her?" wondered Scarlet.

"Of course. And Selena."

"Oh, yes," said Scarlet in reference to the Latin singer who'd died tragically. She shuffled some papers inside her notebook.

"Do you have much homework today?" Tam asked, bringing the bowls of ice cream into the room.

"No, not much," admitted Piper. "There's only four weeks of school left." She gave Scarlet a wistful stare. "You're lucky you don't have to test."

Scarlet shrugged and glanced at the notebook. The cover had a collage of vivid colors. Tam handed Piper her ice cream, then offered Scarlet her bowl with a hand out for the book. "What do you have there?"

Scarlet hesitated, her gaze locked on Tam as if searching for any motive, then she traded the notebook for the bowl of chocolaty ice cream. "It's my sketchbook."

Tam peeked inside. "Oh, that's good." It was an impressive pen-and-ink drawing of a highway underpass covered in graffiti.

"It was near where I lived," mumbled Scarlet. "My last house—I mean place. I lived with my mom." She took a small breath as if out of sorts.

Tam sat down on the couch on the other side of Scarlet. There was a sketch of a baby's profile with chubby cheeks and laughing eyes on the next page. It was Jax. "Scarlet, this is amazing," she gasped. The girl sat as frozen as the ice cream in her lap.

"I didn't know you were an artist," Piper chimed in. She slurped a spoonful of the brownie chip.

"Oh, I'm not. I just…" Scarlet cleared her throat. "I like to draw is all."

Tam gave her the stink eye. "Come on, this is brilliant. You know you're good." The girl lowered her gaze. "Claim your gifts, Scarlet. No else is going to do it for you. You are an artist."

"I guess."

"Mom!" blurted Piper. "You said you wanted to do a mural in the tearoom. Something cool." She widened her eyes and pointed at Scarlet.

"Oh, I—" Scarlet shook her head.

Tam hesitated. She'd been thinking of an elegant scene, perhaps quaint, but… The question hung in the air until something nudged her heart, and she knew what she had to do. "Want a job?" she asked Scarlet. The ploy worked.

"Job?" Scarlet stirred her bowl of ice cream, but her tone sounded interested.

"Yes. I'm going to be painting a new store we're opening next to our herb shop. I need help rolling on a base color, and I'm thinking about a mural." Tam glanced at Jax's profile. "Would you like to do the mural?"

"Me?"

"Of course," said Tam. "I had something a little more old-fashioned in mind, but maybe I need to brainstorm before I make any final decisions."

"Kids like tea and healthy drinks, too, Mom," Piper reminded her. "It could be a cool place to hang out for everybody. Not just for fancy tea parties."

"You're right. I need to consider other angles. Maybe I'm thinking too *vintage*." Tam turned back to Scarlet. "I'll show you some of my ideas, and you come up with a couple, and we'll see if we can make it work."

"Okay," she agreed. Her ice cream was melting. She'd sunk into the cushions behind her. "If my father lets me."

"The herb shop is right across the street from the bakery," Piper informed her. "I'll help. I can use a paint roller. We were thinking of green and there'll be white tables."

"That'd be sweet, I guess," said Scarlet with some hesitation.

"You guess?" Tam leaned forward.

The girl took a bite of ice cream. "I mean, yeah, that'd be cool."

"But," prodded Tam.

"Well," she mumbled, "it sounds kind of… regular."

"What would you suggest?" queried Tam.

Could a twelve-year-old create a vibe that would make people from all walks of life feel comfortable?

"I wouldn't do fancy white tables."

"Why?"

Scarlet shrugged. "Kind of…ordinary."

"What kind of place would make you want to hang out and have a snack?" prodded Tam.

"Somewhere with long wood tables and benches. Places to chill."

"That'd be so cool," gasped Piper. Tam arched a brow. "Really, Mom, it would. Rather than do some kind of old tea party thing, you could mix it up. Like a tea lounge more than something fancy-pants."

Tam scrunched her brows. She'd only thought about adults. She tried to imagine a place women would like to gather, men would like to relax, and teenagers would like to hang out. Maybe the girls were right. "I think some vintage dessert tiers would look kind of cool on modern long tables," she mused.

"Yeah, here and there," said Scarlet. She took a bit of ice cream and glanced sideways at her. "Gold walls would be cool, like mustard, with real art and stuff."

Piper held up her spoon like she'd had an epiphany. "We were talking about magnolias and a historical home for the mural, but that's so…"

"Standard," muttered Scarlet.

"How about a barn or a field of flowers?" suggested Piper. Scarlet frowned to herself again.

"That's a starting point," said Tam. "I'm open to a different color on the walls, but let's brainstorm on the mural some more."

"I can do some sketches," Scarlet offered. "There's that park in town with the cool water fountain."

"On the square, yes," said Tam. "That's a great place. It's kind of a Lagrasse landmark."

"And there's the giant old oak called the General's Tree," Piper added.

Tam returned to the kitchen to let the girls chat. Despite their differences, they were getting along. She listened to them talk as she pulled out homemade lasagna from the freezer to defrost for dinner. The television flipped on, and she peeked once to make sure it wasn't something too mature. A knock on the front door made her pivot from the microwave, and she strode to the front door, expecting Patrick and wondering if she should point out that now was a terrible time to let down his daughter. And there he was when she opened it, hair askew, shirt rumpled, with his pale green eyes wide and stricken. A sobbing Jax cried over his shoulder.

Tam's heart went out to the man. He had a full-time job, a baby, and a teenager, and was new to Lagrasse. She'd been wrong to judge him for being late. Before she could offer any more help, he asked, "Where's my daughter?" in a terse voice.

For some reason, Tam didn't feel appreciated or empathetic anymore. Perhaps she should have just stuck to business.

Chapter Five

Patrick had awakened with a start in the back of the bakery. The doorbell must have chimed— a customer leaving after finding no one at the counter. He'd lain beside Jax after things quieted down and must have fallen asleep. One look at the time on his phone, and he saw the text. Panic had rushed through him.

Tam looked nonplussed as she stood at the white door of her little brick cottage with her blouse untucked from her slacks. A lock of hair was pushed behind her ear showing off the constellation of freckles on the side of her cheekbone, but all he could see was gray fog while his mind frothed with guilt.

She motioned over her shoulder with her chin. "She's right here. She's fine." He took a deep breath as Jax wailed. "Do you want me to..." She held out her arms.

"No, I got him. Can I..." Patrick didn't want to barge past her.

"I thought it'd be better to pick her up than to—" Tam began.

"It's okay," he said, brushing her off. It was not okay. He'd overslept. Abandoned Scarlet.

"Are you alright?" Tam held her hands out for Jax. "Let me take him. I don't mind."

"I got him," he insisted, chest squeezing.

Tam took a step forward, close enough to whisper. That near, he could see into her shining eyes. A slight dimple in her jaw appeared when she grimaced.

"Look, the parking lot was emptying, and I didn't want to leave her there. Piper and she are having ice cream and talking."

Patrick nodded. He felt lightheaded.

"I didn't mean to scare you," Tam said in concern. "I know you're protective of her."

"I fell asleep," Patrick admitted in a hoarse tone. He might as well be honest, since she'd done so much for him. Jax continued to whimper. Patrick's back throbbed. "I should have—"

"It happens," said Tam.

"No," he replied. "It can't. Not right now. She needs…" *A father. A mother. A home.*

Tam rested a hand on his arm, a comforting gesture he needed. "Patrick, I don't know a lot about what's going on, but I know she's not upset. Come on in." She took a step back, and when he walked in, she held out her arms with determination. "Let me hold the baby. Please?"

She eyed him. He was being ridiculous. It was shame more than anything. He'd been hard on Scarlet's mother. Maybe there should have been more mercy. He handed Jax over with relief.

"Come on, baby boy," Tam said. "Let's get you a Popsicle." Jax settled down, curious about his new surroundings and Tam's familiar face. As she carried him off, Patrick walked into a small family room with a cozy-looking sectional and television. Scarlet and Piper sat side by side with empty bowls on a coffee table in front of them. Something flitted across his daughter's gaze when she met his eyes.

"Hi, Mr. Butler," said Piper without missing a beat.

"Hey," he said. He put his hands on his hips, mind scrambling for something to say. Scarlet started staring at the TV as if she hadn't just seen him. She sat rigidly, a notebook open on her lap and her hoodie lying beside her.

"Sorry I was late," he began.

Piper said, "We didn't mind bringing her home. We had a little math to do."

"Same math class?"

"No, but we have the same teacher."

"That's nice."

"Yes. Scarlet's going to help us paint the new store," Piper added.

"Oh?" Did she mean Tam's tearoom? Scarlet glanced at him, jaw tight, bottom lip protruding.

"If it's okay with you. Look." Piper eased the notebook from Scarlet's lap and held up the page. There was a sketch of a water fountain that looked familiar.

"That's nice," Patrick relented. "We'll have to talk about it. Get your things, honey, so we can get back home."

Scarlet hopped to her feet, tossing Piper a churlish look. "You mean, Ms. Donna's," she muttered.

"Yes, Donna's," Patrick said, cheeks warming. "For now," he added, hoping he sounded confident. He'd have them a home soon enough.

Tam wandered back into the room with Jax on her hip. The little boy was happily sucking on a red, white, and blue Popsicle that looked like a rocket while she held it for him. "All packed up?" she asked Patrick.

"Yes, thank you for getting her."

"It's no problem." Tam shook her head. "In fact, I can pick her up any afternoon you have to work late."

"No, that's okay," said Patrick in a rush. "It won't happen again."

"I guess I'll see you tomorrow." Piper nudged Scarlet.

"Okay." Scarlet slid her hoodie back on as if it was chilly outside. She avoided eye contact with Patrick, and the tension in the room rose. It was as if she didn't want to leave.

"Thank you," he told Tam. "I owe you."

She raised a shoulder. "This is Lagrasse, and we're practically neighbors. You don't owe me anything."

Scarlet looked embarrassed. "Sorry to be a problem."

"You aren't a problem. I can't wait to see what ideas you come up with."

The girl waved goodbye at Piper, then trudged past Patrick without another word. He sighed and reached for a drooling and sticky Jax. "Thank you," he murmured.

"Everything okay?" Tam asked in a low tone. She escorted him to the door with the pop still in her hand.

"Yes. Let me know if there's anything I can do for you," he began. He knew his tone sounded desperate, but he didn't want Tam to think he couldn't take care of his own children.

"I didn't mean to cause any trouble."

"You didn't," he said. "It's my fault. I should have been there."

"Don't beat yourself up." Tam offered him the Popsicle to hold. She'd made Jax happier, too.

Patrick accepted the sticky thing with a sigh. "You must think…"

"What? That you're a busy dad? I'm a single parent, too. Things happen."

But she was doing an amazing job. He glanced at Piper across the room and wondered if Tam had any idea how angry Scarlet would be with him. "I wish you would have asked me first, though," he admitted. The fear that had hit him had nearly made his heart give out.

"I will next time."

"There won't be a next time. I'll make sure of it."

"Okay, but just so you know, I offered to hire her to help paint the new shop."

Patrick shook his head. He couldn't keep up with Scarlet already between school and the bakery, and he wasn't sure she needed to be painting the competition's store.

"Why not?" Tam's voice had a sliver of demand.

"She needs to stay with me so I know she's okay."

"She'd be across the street, and she'd be with me," said Tam, confused. "I understand if you're not comfortable with that, but you did say you want her to make friends and settle in."

"I don't see how having her underfoot at your business is going to help."

"She likes to draw, and she's talented. I was going to hire someone to paint a mural anyway."

"A mural? She's not even thirteen."

"What's the worst thing that could happen?" He raised a brow.

"Worst case it'll be a conversation piece." Tam shrugged.

Appreciation flooded through him, a strong force that tightened his throat. She was all about her businesses prospering, yet she'd let a young teenager paint a wall in her store? "I'll talk about it with her later," he promised. "And thanks again for picking her up."

She nodded as he stood there, juggling Jax and the Popsicle, feeling helpless and thankful at the same time. "I guess I'll see you later."

"Sure," said Tam. "Feel free to bring her over to the store on Saturday anytime after ten in the morning. I'll be cleaning."

He bit the inside of his cheek at Tam's persistence. Was he shirking his responsibilities, letting his daughter hang out with another parent? He had the bakery to run and the Flavor Festival to think about. "We'll see. Like I said, thanks."

"Like I said, no problem." Tam wiped a string of sugary drool from Jax's lip, and a faint smile creased her cheeks. "You can hand over a bushel of peaches to pay me back." She grinned, and for the first time in several hours, the knot at the base of Patrick's spine relaxed and he chuckled. Despite her teasing and driving ambition, he knew something was true. Tam Rochester was a real peach.

Scarlet didn't speak to Patrick the entire way home even after he apologized for being late. He didn't tell her he'd fallen asleep, and guilt nipped at him for allowing her to think he'd gotten busy at the bakery. After dinner, Donna asked her to help with dishes, and later he found her in the guest room Donna had provided doodling in a notebook while lying flat on her stomach on the bed. Little Jasmine reclined beside her licking her paws.

The small room was simple but cozy, with a nightstand, quilt, and a fuzzy needlepoint rug on the floor shaped like a turtle. A small square window allowed the setting sun over the backyard to fill the room with tangerine light. Donna had urged him to talk with her, to be truthful and open lines of communication. But there were no lines with Scarlet. Just rocks and boulders and giant potholes.

"Hey," he called after a sharp knock. The pen froze in her fingers as if she was holding her breath.

"Come on in," she muttered.

"I'm sorry," he said. "I knocked, but I should have waited."

"I wasn't doing anything wrong."

"I didn't think you were. Did your mom accuse you of that?"

"No....Maybe." Scarlet sat up, swinging her legs to the floor and looking down as if waiting for a lecture. The Siamese cat mewed and climbed into her lap.

"You don't have to get up."

"I know you're going to talk."

"I thought we should have a conversation."

She stared at the rug.

"I'm sorry," he said. "Jax was fussy all day, and when Donna left, I laid down on the floor beside him in the office." She waited. "I fell asleep, and I'm sorry. From now on, I'll set an alarm."

"Okay," she said after a long pause.

"I didn't forget you. I just fell asleep."

"At least you weren't drunk."

"Of course not," said Patrick, startled. It was another pebble of guilt he didn't deserve. "I need you to understand it isn't normal or acceptable to oversleep all the time."

"Okay."

He leaned against the wall, silently urging her to make eye contact. "Scarlet, I love and care about you, and you are important." She opened her mouth to stay something, then clamped her jaw shut. "What?"

She took a deep breath. "Nothing."

"No, seriously. What?"

"It's no big deal. I'm used to being forgotten."

"I fell asleep by accident," Patrick reminded her. "I'm sorry. I made a mistake."

Her eyes glistened, and she looked away. Suddenly, he suspected she'd heard these excuses before.

"Ms. Tam was there."

"Yes, and I appreciate that. It was nice of her to bring you home."

"She's cool," Scarlet said. "She lets Piper have a phone. No internet, but she has a phone."

"We can talk about that," Patrick relented. "I guess it's time we get you something."

His daughter examined him with a long stare. "They invited me to their shop on Saturday."

"Yes, we need to discuss that, too."

"Talk about what?" Scarlet sounded defensive. "It's just across the street from the bakery. She wants me to paint."

"Do you know how?"

Scarlet gripped her notebook, and for a second, Patrick thought she might throw it at him. "I can draw *and* paint."

"Okay." He was impressed at her courage.

"Can I see?" He motioned toward the notebook that she always kept to herself. She stared at him for several long seconds in heavy silence. The wall was still there, its barbed wire sharp, keeping him out. "At least show me your ideas for the mural."

"Fine." She held it out as if she was surrendering a piece of her heart. Patrick realized he'd let her keep that side of her private for too long— the art therapy, the drawings she'd carried with her. Perhaps waiting for her to offer them to him had been a mistake. Perhaps she'd just needed to be asked all along.

"Just the mural," he assured her and, ignoring the outstretched hand, he crossed the room and sat down by her on the bed. "Show me," he encouraged her, "and I'll tell you my plans for the bakery. It's pink, you know."

A laugh escaped from the back of her throat. "It looks like a bottle of calamine lotion exploded. Lame."

"I think it's okay." Patrick chuckled. "But maybe a coat of white would tone it down."

Scarlet flipped open a page of the notebook. There was a sketch of a water fountain with a beautiful tree in the background.

"Hey," mused Patrick as he took the notebook from her. "I've seen this before. I take Jax to the park to play here." She watched him breathlessly as one small hand rubbed Jasmine on the head.

"This is really good." He studied the artwork, imagining it as a mural on a wall.

"Thanks," came a whisper from beside him. It didn't come out a hiss. Patrick exhaled as a protective barnacle fell off his own heart. "So about a new phone…"

Tam tried to keep it business as usual at The Gracious Earth on Tuesday, but when the store was quiet she couldn't resist running next door to Petal and Pies to measure for the change of plans with the tables. Scarlet had been right. Using long tables would not only look different, but they'd provide more seating. It'd also feel cozy and trendy. Bar height tables along the front windows would provide a great view for single customers who just wanted to sip and see. The rest of the tearoom could be accented with cozy loungers and two person settees against the walls. Old and new. Yesterday and today. It seemed to go perfectly with her new tea line. She'd provide traditional popular brands, and her own line would be unique and edgy. Young and old coming together.

Her stomach rumbled as she rang up two bottles of vitamins for retired schoolteacher, Monk Coles, then waved him off. Across the street, people were entering and leaving The Last Re-Torte in a steady stream. She wondered if they were sold out of hand pies for the day. The small salad she'd eaten at lunch had not filled her up.

Brushing off her blue jeans, Tam checked her hair in the mirror in the back office, then reached into her purse for tinted lip balm. No use in not feeling fabulous. It was not because she was venturing across the street, she told herself, then tiptoed out of the store after flipping over the Out to Lunch sign. She was just going for a light snack. Suddenly, she wondered if the commercially produced pies for her tearoom would be enough.

With a deep breath, she crossed the street and breezed through the door, inhaling the wonderful smell of bread. Donna was at the register. She waved, rang up two loaves of bread for Mr. Carter from the newspaper office, then beckoned Tam forward. "Hello, Gracious Earth. Thank you for gracing us with your presence today."

Tam laughed. "I thought I'd have a peach pie with my tea. Any left?"

Donna reared back and scanned the bakery shelves. "Looks like two." She pointed. "But let me see what's happening in the back. Patrick's handling the workload." She disappeared before Tam could protest, so she tapped her fingers on the counter eyeing the morning's muffin selection.

"Hey."

She looked back at the register in surprise, heart vaulting over a fence she'd put in place long ago. Patrick had a white oxford on, sleeves rolled up, with khaki pants coated in granulated sugar. There was a streak of white dust on his lower jaw, and her hand twitched with an urge to reach out and wipe it off. "Uh, hi," she said, hoping her tone sounded polite—not fascinated, curious, or pleased to see the man who'd acted like she'd interfered rescuing his daughter the day before. "Donna was just checking—"

"More hand pies. We just took them out of the oven. Would you like a warm one?"

He didn't seem upset about Scarlet anymore. "Of course." Tam studied him. "You look like you're doing better."

"It's been a good day."

"Things are okay with Scarlet?"

He swiped at his jaw as if aware it was dusty. "Um, yeah. I want to thank you for that. I'm sorry if I was short. It was a little embarrassing."

"It's fine. You were frazzled."

"I felt awful. I'm not used to being late *or* frazzled." He gave a self-deprecating chuckle. "Did you know there's not a recipe for single parenting?"

"I did." She smiled. "That's why I said not to worry about it. You're in Lagrasse. The right people will have your back."

"Well, thanks for having mine, despite…" He glanced toward the window to the street.

Tam thought about the blank wall in Petal and Pies that would look interesting with a mural. "Did you decide if you'd let Scarlet do the mural? I'll pay her. It's tax deductible."

Patrick met her eyes. "If you insist. I know she's excited about it. Eager, anyway."

"Sometimes eager is the only way some people can show their excitement," said Tam. "I'm sure she has reservations, but this could help her come out of her shell."

"You're kind to offer," said Patrick. "I should have been paying more attention to the things she spent her time doing, like reading and drawing, instead of how she was reacting to everything."

"Reading is a great escape," Tam reminded him. "Be aware of what she's into and read some books with her."

He raised his brows. "I never thought of that."

"It'd give you something to talk about. You could fan girl with her."

He laughed. "Thanks. You're full of advice."

"I have a girl. I'm a girl." She shrugged, but she was flattered by his compliment.

Donna came around the corner with a sleepy-eyed Jax on her hip and a bag in the other hand.

"Warm pie for you!" she called over a loud buzzing from the back.

"Oh!" exclaimed Patrick. "He's awake."

"And ready for lunch." Donna looked back over her shoulder. "And that buzzer on the top oven is stuck yet again."

Tam's heart skipped at the sight of the blue-eyed adorable baby. "Hi, Jax," she cooed, aching to take him into her arms. Jax smiled and pointed as his father took him. "I'm coming!" Donna called to the timer in the back and darted away.

Patrick tapped in something on the register, and Tam dug her card out of her wallet. "You all make a good team." The buzzer in the back was silenced.

"It's trickier than I thought with Gretchen no longer working except Saturdays or emergencies. Donna and I tag team the best we can, depending on my schedule and how she feels."

"What about hiring anyone new?"

"I'm working on that so Donna can step back more."

"You have Scarlet," suggested Tam.

He winced. "She can't boil water. She hasn't been taught."

"Now's a good time," Tam pointed out.

Patrick hesitated. "I just hate to ask her. She's had so much responsibility already."

"Well, she'll still need some." Jax began to whimper. "Oh, poor guy, are you hungry?" Tam let Patrick slide her card and waited for him to hand her a receipt. The buzzer in the back kitchen went off again. Patrick groaned. "I better get him fed before—"

"Oh, no!" Donna screeched. "The short in that thing is driving me crazy!"

"That oven!" Patrick huffed in exasperation. "It has a mind of its own."

"Like teenage girls," Tam chirped with a grin.

Another customer came through the door. "Patrick!" Donna called over the buzzer. Jax began to cry. "I'll be with you in a moment," Patrick said to the newcomer. Tam gave him a wave just as Jax began to scream. He tensed and looked over his shoulder.

"Here. Let me," said Tam. She reached across the counter, and Jax sailed into her arms.

Patrick's gaze swung from the customer to the back kitchen. "Go," Tam shooed him. "Jax and I will be across the street," and without waiting for him to protest, she walked out the door, bouncing the precious baby on her hip and promising him pieces of her peach pie.

Chapter Six

It took more than an hour for things to quiet down at The Last Re-Torte. The oven buzzer was disassembled, customers, including a trio of firefighters, were served, and the counters were cleaned. As Donna headed to the back with the books, Patrick took the last two muffins out of the case and packed them away. He checked the time. There was only an hour before school pickup, and he had to go across the street and get Jax. It felt odd not having his little boy nearby, but Donna had reminded him that Tam was a responsible, loving adult and well respected in Lagrasse. If she had minded, she wouldn't have offered. It filled him with gratitude.

Patrick strode out into the sunshine, inhaling late springtime air that filled him with a contentment he hadn't felt in months. Tam was right. He needed to let Scarlet paint the mural, no matter the outcome. It was something she believed she could do. Who was he to tell her otherwise?

He stepped into The Gracious Earth, appre-

ciating the ambience. Handwoven rugs with or-
anges and reds lined the wood floors. White
shelving units filled with vitamins and herbs
sat against light green walls. Teak displays held
books, honey jars, and other local goods. Across
the other side of the room, glass canisters were
filled with dried flowers and leaves. Soothing,
delicate flute music floated in the air. It smelled
like he was in a deep, dark forest glade.

Patrick walked up to the counter and looked
around. He found Tam and Jax sitting on a
blanket on the floor at one end of the register's
counter. The baby was playing with unlabeled
vitamin bottles that rattled when he shook them.
Tam caressed his dark locks and looked up at
Patrick with a soft smile.

"I assumed that would be you. All is well with
the world," she said in a low tone.

"It looks like he's settled down."

"We shared a peach pie."

"Vitamins?" Patrick motioned at the makeshift playthings.

She shook her head. "Just making do. Empty
bottles with a few pennies inside. He can't get
them open. They're childproof."

The stress of the day floated away in Tam's
makeshift woodland. Patrick sank down onto the
edge of the blanket. "Sorry it's late."

"It wasn't a problem," she assured him. "It helped pass the time, and visitors love him."

"Yes, he charms the bakery customers, too. Captain Hollister from the firehouse calls him our mascot." Patrick's cheek twitched. "I need to pick up Scarlet and get her home, so I better collect this little guy."

Hearing his voice, Jax looked up at him and grinned. "There's Da-da," cooed Tam.

Jax glanced up at Patrick and gave him a drooling, toothy grin. "Da-da," he repeated with gusto.

Patrick sat back in surprise. Tam laughed. "He knows your name."

He shook his head. "Donna's been browbeating him with it. Scarlet's hard to say, so they're shooting for 'sis.'"

"Well, Da-da has sunk in," chuckled Tam.

"I've never heard it before," he said, clearing his throat to keep from sounding emotional.

"Da-da," said Jax again and crawled to his lap. Patrick picked him up and held him.

"Hi, Jax," he said, not bothering to hide a grin.

"Scarlet never said Da-da?" Tam wondered. Cross-legged, she leaned back on her hands.

"No," admitted Patrick. "Scarlet was a late talker, and I—I didn't get to see her much after she was two or three years old."

"I can tell that was rough on you."

"She was little, and her mother wouldn't put her on the phone if I called. I usually wasn't allowed to see her. They were always busy, whatever."

"I'm sorry." Tam studied him. "It's the other way around for Piper."

"What do you mean?" He inclined his head with interest.

The independent woman raised a shoulder as if it didn't matter. "Her father didn't want to be a father—or a husband—after the first year. We married quite young, and his heart wasn't really in it."

"I don't understand that."

"Neither did I," Tam admitted. "It's just been her and me and…" Tam flushed. "Well, I was in a relationship with a great guy a few years ago, but Eric decided to move to Chicago for work."

Patrick raised a brow. "That's quite a distance."

"He didn't want us to come. It was a job opportunity, and he wanted it more than…" Tam sat up suddenly. "It doesn't matter. I have Piper, and she has me."

"It's wonderful you're so close."

"She's my first priority. I try to make sure she's always happy and that we get along."

"I can only hope to have that with Scarlet someday."

"You will," Tam promised before quieting

again. "But they grow up. Leave home. Someday Piper will…" Her voice caught, and it punched Patrick in the chest. He'd never seen her look so serious.

"You're afraid of losing her," he observed.

Her head gave a small nod. "I try to live every day making sure she wants to stay in my life." She looked up at him. "I know you're just getting to know Scarlet. You've already lost her once. But the thought of Piper moving on fills me with dread. I mean, I'm excited for her to fulfill her potential, but the thought of being on my own without her makes me feel…"

Patrick nodded. "I've been there. Since my mom passed, everyone in my family spread out. I know now family's worth fighting for. That's why I'm here. Donna understands. She's always been there for me."

"That's how it's been with my cousin, Ali. " Tam reached out and brushed a finger down Jax's cheek. Before she dropped it in her lap, Patrick reached for her hand and squeezed it.

"Look, if there's anything I've learned from this mess I'm trying to sort out, it's that whenever someone closes a door on us, God always knows another way out. I'm lucky to have Donna and her family. They're an answer to my prayers." He exhaled. "My dad is older, frail, and he lives with my brother up north. I couldn't put this on them right now, and something about Lagrasse has always felt right."

"Yes," Tam mused, "life has a funny way of doing that. We're from Columbus, but Lagrasse has become my true home. And that means keeping the herb shop afloat. Opening the tearoom will help a lot."

"You deserve it," said Patrick sincerely. "I've never seen anyone work so hard. You're brave, you take chances, and you bring everyone with you to the table. Like selling your cousin's honey. Or helping with Scarlet." Now, if she would just make room for the bakery he needed to succeed.

"I try," she admitted. She smiled and the cleft in her freckled cheek flashed.

It struck Patrick in the heart like a fiery javelin. He set down Jax on the blanket and busied himself with checking the time on his phone. "I better go get her."

"Yes, me, too," smiled Tam. "Piper, I mean."

"Do you want me to pick her up?" he blurted. "There's no use in us both going the same way every day."

Tam shook her head. "Donna lives a ways out, and you'd have to come back to town."

"I don't mind," Patrick assured her. "It's the least I can do since you kept Jax. I'll pick her up today, and you can wrap up what you need to here in the shop."

"If you're sure. You're not closing?"

"No. Donna is taking care of things. She has a meeting with her accountant." Patrick stopped short. He might as well tell her. "Things are going better than expected at the bakery, but unfortunately her pain is worse."

Tam's eyes rounded. "Is she okay?"

"She just has to slow down sooner than expected." Patrick cleared his throat. "So rather than wait, I'm going to sign the papers soon and have the grand reopening during the Flavor Festival after all."

"Oh." Tam's lips let it slip out like it burned, then she sealed them shut. "That's wonderful," she stammered. "Congratulations."

"You, too," he returned, hoping she understood. "I should bring Scarlet by on Saturday to paint, right?"

Tam nodded, but her eyes held a faraway look. "Sure. Yes. Saturday."

Patrick hoped he was doing the right thing for his daughter, although the woman across the street thought he was in her way. And the truth was, she was in his.

Ali showed up at the house the next afternoon while Tam was chopping dill, romaine, tomatoes, and cucumbers for a salad.

"That looks delicious. From your garden?"

"The romaine, yes. Tomatoes and cucumbers aren't quite in," Tam replied.

"Delicious." Ali pulled a chair out and collapsed into it. "Heath has the kids, and I'm supposed to be picking up pizza at Pizza Pies even though I have a whole garden of vegetables."

"Lucky you." Tam smiled.

Ali leaned over the table and clasped her hands. "What gives? You said Patrick Butler's doing a grand reopening?"

Tam set down the knife on the cutting board and sighed. "Yeah. Sorry about the late-night text. He told me Donna is going to quit soon, and he wants to do a grand reopening on the day of the Flavor Festival."

"On your opening day."

"Yes. Business has picked up there. What happens when I have pies to sell?"

Ali raised a brow. "I think maybe it's just the peach pies."

"I feel terrible Donna is worse," murmured Tam. "I just didn't expect the bakery to stay open, much less have a grand reopening on the same day as mine."

Ali reached for a sliced cucumber and popped it in her mouth. "How are things going for Petals and Pie?"

"The interior design plans have changed since Scarlet Butler is going to paint the mural. She didn't seem crazy about my dark green palette, and the white tea tables are out."

"You already have a green herb shop. What does she have in mind?"

Tam shrugged. "Yellows and creams? She said she'd bring her ideas over Saturday. I'll at least get primer on the walls, and she can start sketching."

"What can I do?"

"Thanks for offering, but I think the girls and I have it taken care of for now. I'll have Piper work on the counters, and we'll sit down together and order the tables and chairs. I picked out new ones."

"It sounds like it's going to be wonderful," mused Ali. "Warm and friendly. I look forward to having somewhere to meet and chat besides McDonald's."

"Yes, me, too." Tam smiled. "It never occurred to me I'd attract a younger crowd, though, so that's kind of exciting."

"I know you love that." Ali grinned. "Piper and friends will probably hang out there."

"I'd love it. Did I tell you that I have the preliminary order set up with the commercial bakery in Atlanta? It'll be perfect."

"What about the bakery?"

"What about it?"

"Why don't you order from them?"

Tam frowned. "Because of competition. With my luck Patrick will decide to start selling scones."

Ali chuckled. "I don't think he's that kind of man. I've seen him with his little boy."

"Yes, he's a loving father. Donna adores him. He offered to pick up Piper yesterday, and she texted me earlier he was bringing her home again today."

"And the daughter?"

"She's coming around, I think. Rough life. She and Piper have connected."

"Poor thing." Ali brushed a strand of red hair behind her ear. "If there's anything you need from me, let me know."

"The dehydrated honey is on my list for sure," Tam informed her.

"Is it selling?"

"A little bit," admitted Tam, "but I'll buy in bulk for the tearoom for sure. It'll be great to have it on the tables with other sweeteners."

"That's a wonderful idea," Ali agreed.

"How's it sell at your booth at the Farmers Market?"

"It does okay, but most people want it fresh. Sales will pick up soon with the weather warming."

Tam nodded. Honey season was just around the corner—not to mention blueberries and early summer vegetables. "My lavender is growing like crazy. I'll have plenty for the peach tea this year."

"Wonderful." Ali wrinkled her forehead. "You know, it's just a short walk from the park. You may want to consider some juices for the littles in the tearoom."

Tam inclined her head. "I didn't really think of that. I've gone from ladies and gents to teen-agers. Now children?"

"It'd be nice to have a place where anyone can relax and get to know other people, even busy moms."

Tam smiled. Her cousin's enthusiasm gave her confidence that she was doing the right thing. As if reading her mind, Ali teased, "Maybe you and the baker across the street can get to know each other better, too."

"Oh, no," said Tam. Her cheeks flamed, much to her annoyance. "Our daughters are friends, and we've carpooled out of necessity. Besides, he has a baby boy. Other than that, well…" She scrambled for more facts. "He's a cat guy!" she blurted.

Ali erupted into peals of laughter as the front door opened and shut. "Mom, I'm home," shouted Piper as if they lived in a sprawling mansion.

"We're right here," Tam chided her.

Piper bounced into the kitchen. "Oh," she said with a grin. She heaved her backpack onto the counter.

"How was school?"

"Three weeks and two days left," said the girl. "We get out before Memorial Day." She glanced at Tam in a serious way, then turned to the fridge.

"Everything okay?"

"I should get going," Ali announced. She jumped up. "Don't worry about things. You've survived this long with the bakery across the street, and he seems like an honest, good guy."

"Who's a good guy?" Piper wondered.

"How was the ride home?" asked Tam, giving Ali the side-eye as she changed the subject.

"Mr. Butler gave me a ride home again," she said, like her mother had no idea.

"I know that. How was it?"

"Fine," said Piper in a halting voice.

She glanced at Ali, who gave them both a wave. "Catch up later," she called.

Her wink said more than words, and Tam fought the automated response that made her want to flush again. Yes, Patrick was a good guy, and gorgeous. He was devoted to Jax, Donna, and his baking, but... The man was a bit of a dreamer and took things hard. Besides, he hadn't expressed any interest in her other than the tearoom, which he was now challenging by reopening on her special day. Why waste time thinking about a baker who didn't trust her with his kids and wanted to run her out of business? It was a no-win situation.

"Mom?" repeated Piper, pulling Tam's head out of her emotional spiral.

"Yes?"

Piper eased out Ali's chair and dropped into it. She took a deep breath. "Don't say anything, but Scarlet drew all over one of the bathroom stalls today in the girls' bathroom."

Tam stopped mixing the salad ingredients in her trusty Tupperware bowl. "What happened?"

"Nothing. I mean, we were talking while I was putting on my lip balm then I heard scratching and saw her do it."

"What'd she draw?" asked Tam.

"Just a dolphin jumping out of water. It was really good, but she shouldn't have done it."

"It's not the end of the world, but you're right."

Piper hesitated a beat, then said, "She used permanent marker. And laughed. She said it was so no one could forget her."

Tam winced. "I'm sorry to hear that. Did you say anything?"

Piper stared down at the table. "No."

"She was just expressing herself," Tam allowed, "but it is destroying school property."

"I know. I just didn't know what to say." Piper looked up with pleading eyes. "Please don't tell anybody. I could get in trouble for not telling on her. I'm class president!"

Tam sighed. "I won't. For now. Has anyone said anything?"

"No, but I'm sure someone will. It's big, and they suspend anyone they catch drawing on desks."

Tam's mind went round and round. "Next time, you need to stand up for what's right. Tell her it's wrong, and that she should do it someplace else."

"Okay." Piper met her eyes. "I'm sorry. I just didn't know what to do."

"Thanks for trusting me with this. It happens to all of us now and then."

Piper nodded, then reached for a cucumber. "I'm going to go do my homework."

"Okay." Tam let her escape to her room and returned to the salad bowl. Was hiring Scarlet a good idea after all? She didn't know the details of what the girl had gone through, and now she'd have her painting a mural in her new shop. How would that go over in town if the behavior worsened?

Tam took a deep breath, thoughts tangled. Patrick had his hands full. And she couldn't let his problems get in the way of hers. She had to get the tearoom ready to open by the Flavor Festival and watch out for her own daughter. She'd just have to deal with Piper's troubled friend with kid gloves—one day at a time. She shouldn't be wasting her time letting her mind—or cousin—sing Patrick Butler's praises.

Chapter Seven

Patrick stayed up late on Friday researching rental properties in the county. He'd been busy the past couple days even with Tam dropping by for a muffin and offering to pick up Scarlet on Thursday. He'd chatted with her longer than he'd intended to about her interesting taste in '80s pop music that Scarlet had bragged about, and when he'd admitted to being a Lionel Richie fan, it began a whole new conversation about their concert-going years.

He was stunned when he dragged himself out of bed Saturday morning and found Scarlet dressed and seated at the table. She was sketching when he walked in with Jax. She looked up, and he swung his head to the percolating coffee on the counter then back to her. She shrugged. "Ms. Donna isn't up yet, so I started her coffee."

"That's really kind of you. She wasn't feeling well last night." Patrick had seen Donna wash down pain relievers in the kitchen before going to bed, but she'd shooed him off when he'd pressed her for reasons why.

"Yeah, I figured."

"You don't drink it, do you?" asked Patrick, mildly concerned.

She shook her head. "Never could afford it."

"You should stick with water. Milk if you need it. Coffee is addictive. No use starting it for no good reason."

She eyed him. "Is that why you don't buy soda?"

"I don't drink it a lot, and I want you and Jax to be healthy."

"Well, I like it, but usually it was just gross water from the sink."

"I'm sorry," said Patrick. "I guess that can be your decision. How about once a week? Anything more you'll have to buy for yourself."

She turned back to her paper. "I don't have any money, though."

"You can babysit eventually. And you'll be getting paid for Tam's mural," he reminded her.

Scarlet brightened. It was the most unguarded expression he'd seen. "Yes." She smiled. "And she said I could come in about ten in the morning or so."

Patrick glanced at the clock on the stove. That's why she was awake. "We have about an hour and a half, so let me throw some pancakes together." He slipped Jax into his high chair and went to work, and for a few minutes, a peace settled over the kitchen that almost felt normal. He knew Scarlet had never been served breakfast in the mornings, and she often ate in quiet disbelief.

After cleaning up, they left Jax with Donna, who was munching on pancakes with peach preserves. Patrick was grateful he only had to work a half day on Saturdays, since Gretchen came in, and Donna wisely kept the store closed on Sundays. He and Scarlet arrived at The Gracious Earth a few minutes before ten. Patrick caught a flitting look of anxiety pass over Scarlet's face but resisted the urge to pat her shoulder. "It's going to be fun," he encouraged her. "I'm sure you'll do great." She mumbled something that sounded like *thanks* and took a deep breath.

"I'll be over at the bakery with Gretchen. When Donna gets in with Jax, I'll come by for you before I take him home." He watched Scarlet take a deep breath and reach for the door handle. "Do you want me to go in with you?"

Donna had volunteered to keep Jax that morning, and although it made him feel guilty for not keeping the baby with him, he'd relented. Jax had done well with Tam, and Donna knew her limits.

To his shock, Scarlet mumbled, "Sure," as she climbed out of the car. Patrick raised his brows, grabbed the keys, and followed her to the front door of the herb shop. She hesitated only for a moment, then glancing back at him, reached for the brass pull and let herself in. Patrick followed close from behind.

"Good morning," chirped Tam from a step stool. She held a jar of honey and looked like she'd been up for hours and accomplished a great deal. Her bangs were pulled back with a red bandanna, her eyes sparkled, and she wore a pink button-down shirt with the sleeves rolled up. It was knotted around a waist that he could span with his hands if he wanted to. Her old blue jeans had paint streaks and a few threadbare spots.

"Hi," said Scarlet. She cleared her throat, sounding nervous.

"Welcome. Piper's already next door," said Tam. "I'm just restocking for the day."

Patrick caught himself rocking on his heels as Scarlet passed Tam her notebook.

"Let's see what you got." Tam carried it to the register's counter and leaned on her elbow as she perused a few pages. "I still love the fountain," she said. "And I really like the tree and the abstract human figures in the background."

"They're just people I've seen," said Scarlet.

Tam tapped a few sketches. "I think it'd be great if you could work in families picnicking, children playing, and..." She hesitated and looked up with a grin. "This furry baby here looks familiar."

"It's Jasmine," admitted Scarlet. "She's my cat."

"I see."

Patrick stretched up on his toes. Sure enough, nestled under a bench was a brown-and-gold Siamese cat watching the action.

"That's a good likeness," he said in amazement. The eyes were unmistakable, but not the watchful, lonely expression. That looked more like it belonged to his daughter.

Tam glanced up at him. "I think you've got an artist on your hands."

He smiled but didn't miss Scarlet's snort of self-deprecation. Tam waggled a finger at her. "Hey. Remember what I said about claiming your talents?"

Scarlet gave a modest chuckle. "Here." Tam dipped behind the counter and handed her a set of brand-new charcoal pencils and paintbrushes. "Why don't you head over next door to Petals and Pie? Piper is taping off the walls, and I'll be over in a minute."

"Okay," said Scarlet in a timid tone. She accepted the brushes and gave Patrick a small, fleeting smile when she walked past him for the door.

He watched her leave and turned back to Tam. "I really appreciate you doing this."

"She earned it," said Tam. "I really wanted to have a mural, and she has the talent."

"Well, thank you. I can tell it means a lot to her."

"I hope *you* don't mind," said Tam. She picked at a pile of flyers on the counter as if uneasy.

"Why would I mind?"

"Because you're buying the bakery and you need her."

He raised a brow. "You heard I'm painting over the pink?"

Her mouth dropped. "No. You are?"

"Please don't tell Donna. I haven't told her yet."

"Why?" said Tam as if aghast.

"It's just not my color," he sputtered.

She threw back her head and laughed. He grinned at her contagious mood. "Well, thank you for letting your daughter help me with my project."

"No problem." He smiled. "I've seen a change in her this week. She's softened a little. She's more agreeable."

Tam hesitated as if she wanted to say something, then shook her head. "Good. It's going to take time, though. Teenage girls are complex creatures, so be patient with her."

"I will."

Tam leaned over and heaved one bucket after another onto the counter. "I guess Piper and I will be rolling the primer. I'll get the rest of the walls painted when I'm sure about the color. They talked me out of green."

"Let me help you with those," offered Patrick. The clock was ticking, but helping her carry paint over next door was the least he could do before he relieved Gretchen.

"Thanks." She grabbed two more, circling the counter to join him as he swung the paint cans off the counter. "Follow me," she said rather gleefully.

"Who's going to watch the herb shop?" Patricka asked.

"I'll keep an eye on it from next door," she called over her shoulder. "We're going to put in a door to connect the two stores right there behind the tea canisters, and I'm going to have a second entry in the back."

"That'll be nice," approved Patrick. "Two businesses in one." She sure knew what she was doing. He admired her, but he also wondered if he should be worried.

Tam put down a can of paint and pulled the front door open, catching it with her knee, and Patrick reached over her as she leaned down to pick the paint up. When she straightened, they were nose to nose with their hands full, a tangle of knees and elbows. The appealing fragrance of something soft and floral floated over his senses. Patrick's heart whirled like a Ferris wheel out of control, then fell to his knees. He locked them, amazed they might buckle if he didn't and realized he was still staring into her eyes.

He cleared his throat and looked away as she stumbled backward, dropping one of the cans. "Oh!" she cried, and chased after it as it rolled away. She laughed at herself, picking up the can before it went any farther into the street. "Good thing the lid didn't come off." She exhaled, holding it up to check for damage.

Trying to collect himself, Patrick let the door ease shut and stood there helpless, holding his two cans like they were a lifeline. The smell of sugar and yeast from the bakery across the street whisked away the soapy perfume that had hypnotized him. "I'm glad it's okay," he managed to say. She opened the door to the tearoom and held it for him, and he strolled in as if they had not just had a bizarre, magnetic exchange. His pulse hummed like a mixer when he breezed past her. Piper and Scarlet were speaking in low earnest tones in front of a blank wall.

"Paint's here!" called Tam from behind him, like they'd brought pizza.

The girls stopped whispering about Scarlet's

new phone and stared. Patrick held up his two buckets. "Better get these so I don't start painting and forget the bakery."

Piper laughed and hurried over, oblivious that he'd just had the wild fleeting thought to kiss her mother. He needed to get back to the kitchen, get his hands into some dough, and forget about the feelings that had softened yet another crusty shield around his heart. He had bread to bake, children to raise, and a home to find.

Tam caught herself breathing a sigh of relief after Patrick disappeared. The bakery owner was being too helpful, especially since he was plotting to make the most of the Flavor Festival. She cranked up the music on her cell phone after getting Piper started with the primer, hoping the old rock and roll tunes would keep her mind on the tearoom. The few minutes she'd spent alone with Patrick juggling the paint had been more than comfortable, like the cozy time they'd spent on the floor earlier with Jax. For some reason, standing toe to toe at the door with his light green eyes appraising her had charged her pulse like an electrical current. She groaned under her breath. Letting herself consider him as anything more than Scarlet's father and the business owner across the street would be a complication none of them needed.

The girls had double her enthusiasm, and the work carried on quickly even with Tam darting next door every time they heard the chimes announce a customer dropping by. When Scarlet approached her to refill the paint tray with primer a half hour later, Tam examined the long wall with appreciation, noting there were hardly any drips.

"You've done a good job," she assured her. "The focal wall is probably dry if you want to start sketching." Piper ducked out to go next door for a break and to collect some bottles of water.

"Thanks." Scarlet stood back and examined the wall that would be her canvas.

"Have you ever painted before?"

The girl gave her a sideways glance, and the apples of her cheeks flushed. "Not a mural exactly."

"How about in a class…? Outside?" added Tam thinking of the sketch of the underpass.

Scarlet cleared her throat. "I've painted outside a little, with spray paint."

"Oh," said Tam, suspicions confirmed.

"Some people call it graffiti," admitted Scarlet. "I mean, it is sometimes, but sometimes it's art."

"Art is in the eye of the beholder, I suppose." Tam smiled, then remembered Piper's concerns.

"As long as it's not someone else's property, I guess it's okay."

Scarlet nodded. "I always wanted to paint a room."

"Now's your chance. You have my permission and a purpose. It's to sell tea and pie, and make people want to stay."

"Okay," said Scarlet.

"I mean," continued Tam, mind churning as she tried to be careful with her words, "I wouldn't like it if someone drew all over my walls without asking—in here or in the break room or whatever," she hinted. Scarlet grew quiet. She scratched at a spot of paint on her arm. "I know it's just self-expression, but there's rules—and laws for reasons," Tam added.

"Yeah," said Scarlet more quietly.

"You must think I sound like your dad."

"A little bit."

Tam studied her until she looked. "Adults are obligated to teach what's wrong and right and not just for society's sake. For love. I don't know him as well as you do, but I have to say, he sure seems to love you more than anything in the world."

The girl looked doubtful. Tam raised a brow. "He wanted to be a pastry chef all his life and gave up a chance to work at some fancy place in Miami just to bring you and your brother here. Right?"

"Well, he has the bakery," mumbled Scarlet.

"Yes, that appears to make him happy. Do you think it does?"

"I guess so," Scarlet agreed. "It'll be kind of fun to have a parent that owns a bakery."

"Are you kidding? You'll be one of the coolest kids in town." Scarlet chuckled at Tam's enthusiasm. "He's doing all this so he can get you guys set up in a home here in Lagrasse. Your own place," Tam added.

"I've never really had one," said Scarlet. "A house. I mean, I lived in some rooms at my mom's friends places, and I stayed at my grandma's a few times. Someday I'd like to live in a house. A real one. Just be a real kid."

"You are a real kid. Just make do until it comes true. You hang in there and help your dad out, and before you know it, you guys will have a home of your own." Scarlet stared at the wall as if imagining her sketch, or maybe, a place she could really belong. "I'm looking forward to seeing what you can do," said Tam. "This is the right way to express yourself, and there's art classes. Have you thought about that?"

"Maybe someday," Scarlet murmured.

"You should sign up for the Art Club," Tam suggested.

The girl gave a half nod. "Why not?" she

agreed in a near whisper. "Claim my talent, right?"

"Right."

Piper breezed back in, juggling three bottles of water. "I gave Mr. Coles a jar of honey and he said you have his info."

"I do and thanks." Tam hadn't noticed her regular customer come in next door. She took a step back. "Why don't you start sketching, Scarlet, while Piper and I can look over these paint sample colors."

"I think we've talked her out of green," laughed Piper.

Scarlet grinned. "Purple would be cool."

"I think I'm going to go with the burnt yellow and faux brick behind the counter," said Tam firmly. "This isn't going to be a nightclub." The girls snickered. "And a black accent wall like you suggested." Tam pictured the contrast against the yellow paint and wood floors.

"We should put the mural on a dark wall," said Scarlet before she caught herself.

Tam mulled over the idea. "That's not a bad idea. If you want to go ahead and start we'll paint around it." The girl smiled. "You just may make a name for yourself," Tam added.

Scarlet beamed. "Wouldn't my father be surprised? I'll get the pencils and get started."

Tam felt light as she went for the paint tray.

Yes, Patrick would be pleased, but the tearoom had to be the priority. Especially with the temptations across the street.

Jax dozed during church services on Sunday, content in Donna's arms beside Gretchen, her husband, Rollie, and their girls. Scarlet sat quietly without a scowl. She even smiled at Tam and Piper across the sanctuary of The Good Shepherd Church when they waved. When Patrick left for the bakery Monday morning, his heart was light with hope after hearing about the picture his daughter had sketched on the new tearoom wall, as well as the changes he'd seen in her. He picked up Piper that afternoon, hung around in her driveway talking to Tam until Jax started whining, and she brought Scarlet out to the farmhouse on Tuesday.

Patrick made his midweek batch of peach and strawberry hand pies on Wednesday, punched down Donna's recipe for yeast rolls, shaped them, and fed Jax an early lunch before Donna left to go to the doctor. Afterward, he put the baby in his carrier and let him ride piggyback, hoping he'd sleep, then he frosted the pies before putting the rolls in the ovens.

Soothing music drifted from the store's speakers, and he stopped only when the bells rang, wondering how much longer he could carry the load without extra help. He would need to hire assistants when Donna quit for good. His back couldn't take much more.

Kylee Hollister, a familiar customer, traipsed in, wearing business slacks and a jacket. She was married to the captain at the firehouse, Evan, who dropped by often.

"Donna said you worked in Atlanta?" he queried politely.

"Part-time." The tall brunette smiled. "I had a meeting at the school today with the PTA board."

"Which school?"

"Elementary." She pointed at the fresh hand pies. "I came in for bread, but I'll need a half dozen of those."

"Sure thing." He smiled and turned to bag them.

"Oh, your baby's so sweet. How old is he?"

"Jax is nine months."

"I have six-year-old twins. Actually two sets. Six and one."

"Wow." Patrick almost dropped the tongs in surprise, and she chuckled. "They definitely keep us busy, but we have our routine."

"I don't know how people do it," Patrick admitted. "Work, raise children, keep up with their homes."

She smiled. "It's like crossing an ocean. One stroke at a time with your eyes on the horizon."

He chuckled. She accepted the pastries from him and set two loaves of sourdough bread on the counter to buy as well. "And enjoy the breeze while you're at it. The sunshine, too."

Patrick nodded in agreement. Lord knew he'd had enough storms in his life. Jax and Scarlet, as well. "Thanks."

She tutted at Jax, then said, "There's no way I could work with a little at my side so you're one step ahead of me."

"It's tough, and I'm not sure it's fair to him. I'm going to have to consider childcare in the long run, although it makes me uneasy."

Kylee smiled brightly at him. "You don't have to worry around here. We have Starfish Friends at the church preschool, and several stay-at-home moms babysit."

"Any recommendations?" asked Patrick.

"Ali Underwood, hands down," said Kylee. "She keeps my toddlers and helped with my older kids before they started school."

He narrowed his eyes as red hair and an energetic smile popped into his brain. "Oh, that's right. Ali. Tam's cousin. I see her at the park a lot and she comes in."

"Yes. That's her."

"I thought she was a beekeeper."

"Beekeeper, gardener, dog sitter, babysitter, Super Mom, you name it."

He laughed. "I'll keep her in mind, and talk to her next time she comes in."

"Tell her I sent you," Kylee insisted. "And by the way, she and my husband sent me here. Everyone knows the bread is the bomb, but your pies and the new bear claws are all the rage."

Patrick smiled at the compliment. "I've made my share of bear claws. I can make them in my sleep."

Kylee wagged her head. "I couldn't make a pastry to save my life, but I make a mean pot of soup."

He grinned. "Practice makes perfect, and soup is good food."

"But who has the time?" she teased. She held up the bag and hurried out with a wave. Patrick grabbed a towel to wipe crumbs off the counter. A good sale, an interesting customer, and a new acquaintance with a childcare referral. It was progress. Foot traffic slowed to nothing, and it gave him time to clean a display case. Then the phone behind the counter jangled, and he jumped, realizing that Jax had drifted off to sleep cocooned against his back.

Patrick snatched up the receiver before it sounded again. "Hello," he said in a soft tone then remembering where he was, "The Last Re-Torte."

"Huh? Oh. Um… Is Mr. Butler there?" crackled a stern voice.

"Yes. This is he."

"Mr. Butler, this is Mrs. Skeen at Lagrasse Middle. Mr. Abbott would like to speak with you as soon as it's convenient."

Mr. Abbott? The principal? "Oh, um…" Patrick's mind fogged over. He'd already had Scarlet's records transferred. "I can be there after school when I pick her up."

"Yes, that will work if it's the earliest you can make it," said Mrs. Skeen, who sounded no-nonsense. "It's about Scarlet. She's sitting in the office here."

The office? His heart hurdled past his pulse. "Is she sick?"

There was a pointed pause then, "I'm afraid your daughter has gotten into some trouble, Mr. Butler. If you could get here sooner than later, that'd be best."

"Of course," said Patrick, fumbling with the phone as his cheeks heated, turning his stomach. "I'll—I'll be on my way as soon as I can. It may be up to an hour."

The school secretary disconnected the call. Patrick took a sharp breath, inhaling the scent of baking rolls in the oven along with his disappointment. Heat prickled his skin like thorns. *And so it begins.* The therapist in Florida had warned him to expect issues. But so soon? And she'd been doing so well. He wondered why she hadn't texted him with her new phone.

Jax shifted in his sleep from inside the carrier, and Patrick scanned the bakery shelves he'd spent all morning replenishing. Everything was fresh, some things still warm. He needed to leave right away, especially after being so late picking up Scarlet once before, but he couldn't close. The store wasn't busy, but anyone could walk in at any time, and he didn't want to have a reputation for not always having the doors open, especially with all the talk going around of Donna passing the torch. He groaned. Scarlet needed him. So did The Last Re-Torte.

He glanced out the window, and his heart sank. His best hope was across the street, but she'd already saved him more than once.

Chapter Eight

Tam reached into the safe for Ali's check, then locked it back. She traipsed back to the register fluttering it in the air. "Thanks for bringing the last of your crop in. How about we decide on a count for the tearoom?"

"You want dehydrated, right?" Ali let go of Alice's hand. "Don't touch."

"For the tables," nodded Tam. She rested her elbow on the herb shop's counter and planted her chin on it. "I'm going to need an extra quart or two for behind the scenes."

"For pie?"

Tam flitted her gaze past her cousin's shoulder to the window framing the bakery across the street. "Those will come from Atlanta," she reminded her. "I've decided to order scones, too, to go with cookies from the UK."

Ali murmured, "As long as they're fresh."

"Look," sighed Tam. "It's all about the beverages. I don't have the time or talents to run a restaurant. It's just teas and basic coffee with delectable treats—that someone else will have to put together. I can't do everything by myself."

"Knowing your limits is important, and everyone's excited," Ali assured her. "It'll be nice to have a quiet place to sip and chat, read maybe. Business in the herb shop will probably pick up, too."

"Yes," nodded Tam. "Especially with the park around the corner and the library a few blocks away."

"*And* if they don't want a warm cup they can purchase it loose and take it home." Ali turned up her palms. "Win-win."

"Exactly." Tam smiled.

The front door swung open. Patrick Butler strode inside with Jax in his arms and a diaper bag crossed over his chest. "Hi," called Tam in surprise.

"Hey." He looked like he was in a hurry—and stressed out.

"Is everything okay?"

Ali put a hand on her hip. "Who's minding the bakery?"

"Oh, uh…"

Tam came around the counter in concern. "What's wrong?" She studied Jax. The baby looked sleepy but content. The nasal saline solution she'd offered seemed to have helped his allergies.

"It's Scarlet." Patrick sighed. "Her principal called. I'm not sure what's wrong, but I doubt it has anything to do with the weekend."

"I hope she's okay."

"Me, too. I need to run over to the school right now."

Tam glanced past him. There was no way she could run over and mind the bakery. She had her own business. She was already running back and forth between the Gracious Earth and the tearoom. His gaze briefly connected with hers. "Do you want me to take Jax?" Tam offered. Her heart yearned to hold him.

Patrick exhaled, and his taut, broad shoulders relaxed. "Yes. I hate to ask, but I don't know what's going on or how long it's going to take."

"No problem."

"I would have been happy to," said Ali. Alice released a small shout of exultation from the floor where she was rolling around singing a nursery rhyme.

Tam chuckled. "I got the little guy."

Patrick eased Jax into her arms as if the baby were a kitten, then handed her the diaper bag. "He may go back to sleep."

Tam managed to keep her face neutral, at the ripple of energy that traveled up her arms when he came into contact with her. She wondered what it felt like for Jax, to be cuddled in Patrick's arms, warm and safe. She cast her eyes to the floor and took an abrupt step back. The past two men she'd once wanted to cuddle with had shortly found other priorities. "I'll sit and rock him here for a while."

"Thanks," he said, oblivious to her unreasonable feelings.

"Um-hmm," she mumbled, tongue tangled at the back of her throat.

"I'll be back as soon as I can."

"We're heading across the street," said Ali, breaking the spell. Tam glanced at her cousin, praying her cheeks weren't rosier than usual. "If I see anyone try to walk in, I'll tell them Gretchen is on the way," Ali promised Patrick.

"Great. Thanks." His harried demeanor faded, and he turned back to Tam. "Call me if something comes up, please."

She nodded, impressed he'd asked for help. He gave Jax a soft pinch on the apple of his chubby cheek and hurried out. Ali watched him go, then turned back to the register, one copper eyebrow raised over a hazel eye. "Wow, he's juggling a lot. How is he going to operate a bakery without Donna?"

"I don't know," murmured Tam. "He isn't usually one to accept assistance." She smacked a kiss on the top of Jax's head without thinking, inhaling the soft amber and musk fragrance of baby shampoo that flipped a switch in her ovaries. Taking a step backward, she settled onto her stool with the baby in her arms. "Maybe Scarlet will help out," she supposed.

Ali glanced at the wall between the shop and next door. "How did the mural go this weekend?"

"You'll have to sneak over and take a peek," said Tam. "She has it sketched out, and it looks cool. Almost like a city seal, if LaGrasse could ever lay claim to being that size."

"That's awesome. It's good of you to let one of the locals paint it."

"I think it'll be charming. It's the fountain and General's tree, with pines in the background and a border around it made of peach blossoms."

"It sounds perfect. And not too funky," noted Ali with a grin. "I know you were a little worried."

"Scarlet's observant," noted Tam. "Empathetic. Probably gifted. But troubled."

"You'd have to be to survive what it sounds like she's gone through and keep up with an education."

"You're not wrong," agreed Tam.

"I wonder what's up at the school." Ali collected her check from the counter and glanced at her daughter, who was spread-eagled on one of the rugs, talking to the ceiling.

"Maybe she isn't feeling well," said Tam.

They'd spent all weekend together. She hoped it wasn't catching.

"Well, he did mention the principal. It must be serious."

"I didn't think of that." Tam tightened her hold on Jax, who leaned his head on her arm. She couldn't imagine Scarlet getting into real trouble. She was quiet, even bristly at times, but not a troublemaker. Then she remembered Piper's story about the bathroom graffiti.

"Oh, no," mumbled Tam softly to her cousin. "I think I may know what this is about."

Patrick hurried through the brown double doors and into a yellow-brown lobby with its trophy case, potted palm, and a maroon sofa that had been around since *The Golden Girls*. He let himself into the school's office through a glass door and waited for the secretary to finish tapping on the computer. She looked over a pair of pink-and-blue mottled glasses at him, a curious glint in her eyes. "Can I help you?"

"I'm Patrick Butler."

"Oh." A welcoming smile became more serious. She turned her chin to look down a short hall. "Around the corner." She pointed. "Scarlet's on a bench outside his office."

Patrick thanked her with hot cheeks, wondering why he felt like he was the one in trouble.

With a chest as tight as rubber bands, he strode past certificates and portraits on cinder block walls and turned the corner. There was a bench outside a closed door emblazoned with latex letters that read, Principal. Scarlet was sitting with her arms crossed like she was holding her rib cage together so her heart didn't fall out. Her face was pale, but her jaw looked like it was made of steel. She jumped when she saw him, then shut her eyes in a long blink before returning to stare out the window across from her.

"Are you okay?"

She remained silent for a pause, and calming himself, Patrick took a deep breath and sat down beside her. "What's going on, honey?" Patrick cleared his throat, ready for her to fling it all out.

Scarlet swallowed audibly. "Nothing. I don't know. This is lame. I was just drawing."

"During class?"

She shook her head.

He winced. "Nothing outside on the school, was it?"

"No," she shot back.

"Might as well tell me now," Patrick warned.

She exhaled in defeat. "I was cleaning off a picture I drew last week."

"Off of what?"

There was a long pause then Scarlet mumbled, "The bathroom wall."

His eyes widened. "Seriously?"

"It was inside a stall. Just a dolphin." She jerked one shoulder up in a careless shrug. "I saw it today and cleaned it off. Or tried to."

"So you were trying to make it right."

She slowly nodded. "I didn't really think about it, but after working on Ms. Tam's mural I realized I didn't want to be known for drawing in school bathrooms."

"That was a good deduction. Who saw you?"

"I don't know," she mumbled. "I was in class and got called out."

Patrick tried to put things in perspective. "You did the right thing cleaning it off."

"It didn't all come up," Scarlet admitted. "The coach came and got me and accused me of drawing all of the graffiti in there and wouldn't listen. I was trying to fix it between classes."

"At least you were doing the right thing."

Was he doing the right thing? Defending her? Had anyone ever been in her corner? "Look," Patrick whispered, when a voice rose in the nearby room as if someone was getting off the phone. "If you burn the bread, you take responsibility for it, throw it out and start again. You did that, or tried to. But you'll still have to take the consequences—a new batch, a frustrated boss, sometimes an angry customer."

Scarlet shivered. Her eyes glistened with wetness. Patrick slanted his head. "You don't have anything to be afraid of. Courage is admitting a mistake and doing your best to rectify it."

"That's not how it works," she muttered.

"Oh, yeah? How does it work?"

He smiled, trying to calm her nerves. A silhouette appeared at the door, and the doorknob turned. "Don't let them paddle me, Dad," she gasped as the office door opened.

Dad. Patrick's throat constricted as if the bands around his chest had retied around his neck. His eyes stung with wetness that he blinked away. Principal Charles Abbott, he presumed, stood at the door, a towering thin man with a short Afro and eyes set wide apart. His white dress shirt was stained with ink on the wrist above a left hand that could palm a beach ball.

"Mr. Butler," he called out as if they were old friends. "It's nice to meet you. Please come in."

Patrick stood and waited for Scarlet to rise to her feet. She did so slowly, and he put an arm around her shoulders and pulled her to his side before offering his hand to Mr. Abbott. "It's nice to meet you, too. I wish it was under better circumstances."

The man grinned with big, white teeth as he turned to Scarlet. "Yes, I wish it was, too, but I've been wanting to meet Miss Scarlet and have a little chat for a while now, so we'll just kill two birds with one stone."

He motioned at Scarlet. "Come on in, chick-adee." He stepped back into the office. Patrick and Scarlet took their seats, two ladder-back chairs across from a desk full of office supplies and shuffled papers. There was a basketball trophy on a filing cabinet behind Mr. Abbott, a large computer screen off to the side, and a coatrack by the door piled with jackets and hats. He smiled widely again, opened his desk drawer, and slid out a few pieces of chocolate wrapped in silver foil. "I like to eat the elephant in the room before I bite into anything else."

He held out the chocolate, and Scarlet stared in surprise. Instantly relieved, Patrick took two pieces and handed her one. She met his eyes with mild disbelief.

"So Scarlet told me why she thought I was here," Patrick began. Her anxiety was killing him. He glanced around the room in search of a paddle. Surely they weren't still using corporal punishment these days. Or were they? How far would he go to protect his daughter?

Mr. Abbott leaned back in his chair, and it creaked as he popped a piece of chocolate in his mouth. "Let's see if you're right. Two little songbirds reported she was drawing on the walls in the bathroom, and I thought we should have a talk, since there's not enough space for everyone in the school to do that. Besides, it creates problems." He dipped his chin at Scarlet. "Sometimes people don't draw good things. So we prefer to keep the property clean—it looks nicer—and we let our resident artists use the supplies in the art room."

Scarlet's cheeks flamed red. Patrick cleared his throat. "Well, there's two sides to every story as you know," he began, then he realized saving his daughter didn't mean speaking for her. He gave her a long stare. "Go ahead. Tell him what happened."

Scarlet gave him a paralyzed look, her fist on the arm of the chair taunt, and Patrick reached for it. She didn't pull away.

"Okay," she whispered, voice shaking. "The thing is, I like to draw." She swallowed. "I like dolphins."

"So do I!" Mr. Abbott cried in happy surprise. "You'll have to see my picture from the time I got to swim with one in the Caribbean."

Patrick squeezed his daughter's hand, then sat back in his chair. Scarlet allowed a tiny smile to tug on the corner of her cheek, but her eyes still shimmered with tears. "So last week…"

A few minutes before closing, Tam sang to Jax while peering out the window across the street. The bakery had closed early, which meant Gretchen had not been able to stay long. Tam sucked in her bottom lip, hoping that didn't hurt The Last Re-Torte's bottom line. Jax giggled when she began "Row, Row, Row Your Boat" again, and she bounced him on her hip as she returned to the register to lock it up. Her computer blipped with a new email, and she clicked it open. The furniture she'd ordered was already on its way. Excited, she smiled to herself, imagining the finished vision next door. Somehow, she'd gone from a traditional tearoom to a hangout spot that offered teas, coffees, and pies. She'd have to run it by the bank again, but she admitted it suited the neighborhood better. A more formal establishment like Mary Mac's in Atlanta would have been fun, but it would have limited the customers here in Lagrasse. Now everyone would come. No reservations necessary. She was glad she'd been flexible with her vision and thankful for her daughter's and Scarlet's fresh ideas. Now she had to hope that her potential customers didn't decide to just drop by and pickup from the bakery instead. The Last Re-Torte had its loyal base.

Her phone buzzed with an unfamiliar number. She set Jax on the blanket at her feet, and answered.

"Mom?" came a trembling voice.

"Piper! What's wrong?" Concern washed over Tam from her head down to her fingertips at the heartbreaking tone of her daughter.

"Can you come get me?"

"It's a few minutes early. Are you okay?"

"No." Piper sniffled.

"What happened, babe?" she asked. "Where are you?"

"I'm on the phone in the front office. Mrs. Skeen's phone."

"Are you sick?"

"No," said Piper, and then she began to snif-fle, which meant tears were streaming down her cheeks. The thought of her daughter cry-ing among strangers hit Tam in the chest. She glanced at Jax, wondering how she could pack him safely into the SUV without an infant car seat. "What happened?"

"Scarlet yelled at me. In front of everybody. The entire seventh grade hall."

"What?" Tam's mind tangled with confusion.

"She said I told on her. That I snitched on her for drawing in the girls bathroom, but I didn't."

"I know you didn't," said Tam, feeling defen-sive for her.

"She was getting her stuff out of her locker between classes, I guess to go home, and she turned on me and started screaming in front of everyone."

"Oh, no," said Tam. "Was her dad there?"

"I don't know."

Where was Patrick? Tam glanced at Jax trying to pull himself up by clutching the corner of the counter. "I can't come get you early, baby, I'm sorry. I have Jax here. Mr. Butler went to the school."

"Please. Everyone's whispering about me."

"I can't," Tam said. Her throat tightened as her chest pinched with guilt. "Just hold your head high, and we'll figure it out."

"I thought she was going to hit me."

"Scarlet wouldn't do that," said Tam quickly. "She's harmless." But so angry. Tam didn't really know her well or what she'd been through. She had no idea what the girl was capable of doing. "Just sit tight in the office. I'll be there as soon as I can."

"Okay." Piper calmed down. "Thanks."

"Let me talk to Mrs. Skeen," Tam ordered. She'd make sure her daughter stayed safe with the staff. The door chimes jangled. "I'll be there soon," Tam said to the secretary. She hung up and marched with Jax to the front of the store just as Patrick flew in. "What's going on?" she said, fighting to rein in her temper.

He ran a hand through his hair looking worn out and apologetic. "I'm sorry," he said. "I came back as soon as I could."

"And Scarlet?" demanded Tam. She tried to keep her voice calm but knew it held a tinge of blame.

He looked at her curiously. "She's in the car." He motioned toward the window with his head. "She has weekend suspension starting after next week to help clean all of the bathrooms because she graffitied a bathroom stall."

"That's fair," Tam began, but then she remembered her tearful daughter. "What about Piper?"

He crunched his forehead. "What about her? She's not responsible."

Tam exhaled, glancing toward the window. The outline of Scarlet in the small car was visible. She was leaning her head against the car window as if broken. Tam's defensive anger melted a little bit. "I understand there was an altercation in the hallway."

"What?" Patrick looked baffled.

"When Piper got out of math class, she saw Scarlet in the hall, and she accused her of being a snitch."

Patrick groaned. "Oh, no. That doesn't sound like Scarlet, but…"

"You haven't been around her enough to know," Tam pointed out.

Patrick stiffened. "I know my daughter. She's already mortified she's going to be suspended."

"She should be," said Tam.

Something flashed in Patrick's eyes. "She's a kid. She was just drawing. Wrong place, wrong time."

"And the same goes for Piper. And I think maybe 'wrong friend,'" Tam added before she could catch herself. Her mind raced to rationalize her emotions. "My daughter called me for help, and I couldn't be there for her because I was stuck here."

"What are you saying?"

Tam took a deep breath just as Jax came speeding across the room on his hands and knees. He let out a squeal of excitement at the sight of his father. Patrick hurried past her and picked him up.

"Thanks for watching him," he said, tone brittle. "I should have taken him with me obviously."

"I'm saying," said Tam, circling right back to the exchange, "that maybe Scarlet needs some time to work on herself before she starts hanging out with other kids. Maybe painting the mural isn't a good idea right now."

Patrick's cheeks flushed. "Actually, she needs to be around other kids her age and have something to do. But maybe you're right about Piper. Scarlet needs strong influences."

"My daughter is a wonderful influence," Tam shot back.

Patrick ignored her and picked up Jax's blanket

and retrieved the diaper bag in the corner. "Congratulations. We can't all have perfect children."

"I didn't say she was perfect," said Tam, "but she is kind and generous."

"So is Scarlet," said Patrick. "She just doesn't know how to behave when she's up against the wall."

"I understand that," said Tam, trying to calm herself. "I'm just saying… Piper didn't tell on her although we discussed it, and—"

"Wait." Patrick halted on his way to the door. "You knew?"

"Yes, she mentioned it."

"And you didn't think to tell me my daughter was vandalizing bathroom stalls."

"It was one. I didn't think it was that serious."

"But you could have told me."

Tam stiffened. "Yes. I realize I should have brought it up. You had so much on your plate, I didn't think it warranted getting you upset."

"But she's my daughter," articulated Patrick. "Why did you think I didn't need to know?" His eyes flashed with something akin to resentment that hurt Tam's heart. "I've been locked out of everything she's gone through, and I need people in my corner that want what's best for her—and me," he said, flush deepening after he included himself.

Tam worked her jaw, speechless. Had she been

guilty of keeping it between the girls? "Maybe I was trying to earn Scarlet's trust," she admitted in a gruff voice. "Be the cool mom. You're right, I should have told you."

Patrick gave her a sharp nod. "Scarlet's had enough adults in her life trying to be cool. She needs a real mother, not the cool mom. It's the whole reason we came to Lagrasse." He spun on his heel for the door, leaving Tam speechless.

Lagrasse was a special town with people who were good influences, and she was one of them, wasn't she? She liked Scarlet. They'd connected last weekend. They'd talked about art and music, and joked and laughed until Piper had even become comfortable enough to talk about the cutest boys in their grade in front of her mom.

The sketch of the mural was beautiful. It just needed to be painted. Tam sighed. Would that even happen now? She'd practically told Patrick the girls shouldn't be friends. That was a mistake. She'd let her feelings get away from her. She remembered the sound of Piper's pitiful tears. Her daughter had been hurt and embarrassed, but she was going to be fine. The girls had just had a misunderstanding. Tam grabbed her keys and dashed out to the SUV noting the bakery was still closed and that Patrick's car was nowhere in sight.

Chapter Nine

Patrick hardly tasted his dinner for the second day in a row, and by the look on her face, Scarlet was struggling, too. He'd decided not to bring up Piper or the principal's office, and Donna's big pot of spaghetti definitely lightened the mood. Jax coated himself in red sauce while he dug around in a bowl for chopped pasta with his fist. Scarlet glanced at him occasionally with an expression that looked like she was fighting a smile. It gave Patrick confidence things would blow over, but at the same time, the tightness in his chest told him there was more to talk about. Her verbal attack on Piper was unacceptable, and he needed to sort through the landslide of feelings that had skidded over him at the look of hurt on Tam's face.

He'd come to admire Tam. She was focused, energetic, and overly conscientious about others—not herself. Her bright eyes, freckles, and the adorable dimple in the side of her cheek were enchanting. He gulped down a bite of spaghetti and pushed the ruminations away. He had a troubled daughter to deal with, and a bakery to keep afloat that would soon be his.

Patrick pushed his plate back, giving Donna a sideways glance. As if reading his mind, she put her elbows on the tables and clasped her fingers. "How's the spaghetti?" She polled Scarlet.

The girl looked over. "It's delicious. Thanks. Way better than the discount cans we got at food pantries."

"As good as mine?" teased Patrick.

Donna laughed and swatted at him. "I may not be Italian, but I can make a pot of spaghetti. Your mother taught me."

He laughed despite the longing in his heart to see his mom again. "She taught you well."

Donna didn't miss a beat. She looked at Scarlet. "So what happened at school yesterday?" She asked as if she was unclear about the situation, but Patrick had confided in her in the kitchen when Scarlet ran to her room the day before.

His daughter stared at her plate in response. "So," began Patrick to start her off, "Scarlet left some artwork on the bathroom stall and decided to clean it up, which she should have, but someone saw her and thought she was adding graffiti."

"Tattletales," she grumbled.

"Whoever it was did the right thing," said Patrick. "Remember what Principal Abbott said? Sometimes people leave personal information or unkind messages, so they have to have a zero tolerance rule."

"But it was just a picture."

"Maybe the person who saw you didn't look closely. Regardless, it wasn't our property, so when you get right down to it, he's right." She frowned. "I'm proud of you for cleaning it off though," Patrick added. "Helping the janitor out during suspension with a great attitude can change everything. Give them a chance to see you're a good kid." She looked hard at him. "You are a good person," he said.

"It's true," chimed in Donna. "You took care of your mom, your brother and kept your grades up at your other school. And you're as honest as the day is long." Scarlet blinked, surprised at the compliments.

"I know it's not going to be easy," Patrick admitted. "But helping clean the school starting next Saturday and meeting with the school counselor is a great idea."

She flushed. "Everyone will know."

"Everyone will not know," he said gently. "We all have scars, honey. Whether or not you want to advertise them is up to you."

"You know," said Donna, "even I've gone

through some hard stuff. Like with my son, Michael." Scarlet looked at her with interest. "It was embarrassing to have a son get into trouble for cheating and stealing in high school. And just when I thought we'd done everything to help him, he decided partying was more fun than working or getting additional education."

"Like my mom," said Scarlet softly.

"Well, maybe," said Donna. "They're different people. But Michael chose things I don't approve of, so he left." Her voice split at the seams, and she patted Scarlet's hand. "Your mother's choices affected you, but they aren't yours, and they aren't who you are. No one here knows about your past. Your dad's right. It's up to you how much you want to share with people, but the choices you make reflect who you are and who you want to be. So let's see what you're made of."

"Principle Abbot suggested she join the Art Club next school year," said Patrick. "They meet after hours on Wednesdays."

"That sounds fun. You should consider it," Donna encouraged her.

"What do you think?" pressed Patrick.

Scarlet exhaled but met his eyes. "Ms. Tam mentioned it. I guess I could check it out."

"Great." He took a deep breath. "And maybe you can apologize to Piper on Monday."

She looked down. "Maybe I can do it when I go over to Petals and Pie to paint the mural on Saturday."

Patrick glanced at Donna for moral support. More bad news was not what Scarlet needed, but consequences were consequences. "About that." He twirled his glass and studied it so he didn't have to meet her curious stare. "Ms. Tam decided that continuing with the mural probably isn't a good idea."

"Why?" shot back Scarlet.

"Well, honey, Piper was really upset when you shouted at her yesterday."

His daughter's cheeks flushed. "She told you?" Scarlet scowled. "Figures."

"She called her mom, crying," explained Patrick. "She was really upset, Scarlet. It wasn't to get you in trouble, and by the way, she's not the one who turned you in."

"So she says. And now I can't paint the mural."

Patrick's stomach felt like a knot. They'd both ruined things with Tam. And the Flavor Festival wasn't even here yet. It was going to be business versus business with their daughters caught in between. "No, I'm afraid not."

Scarlet jumped from her chair, eyes tearing. "Then what's the point of Art Club?"

"The point," interjected Donna, "is you can hang out with other artists and get the chance to do projects for the school and community. Your art isn't over."

"Let's just put the tearoom on the backburner for now," said Patrick.

"I didn't mean to accuse Piper, I just assumed it was her," complained Scarlet.

"It wasn't, and that wasn't the way to handle it."

"Fine," she retorted. "Can I go to my room?"

"If you need to," Patrick said. "Or you could help me clean up dinner, since Donna made it."

Scarlet wavered as if enduring ripples of indecision. Dropping her chin, she turned on her heel and stomped up the stairs until a door upstairs smacked shut. Donna winced.

Patrick put his hands over his face. "This is not going like I hoped."

"You knew to expect some bumps along the way," said Donna. "Just hold on tight."

"But this makes things with Tam so…" Patrick's face warmed as if the spaghetti had had some heat. Why did he care so much about the herb shop owner?

"She'll be okay," said Donna. "So will Piper. Taking her over to the tearoom on Saturday to apologize might be a good idea."

"Do you really think so?"

"Yes. You can tell Tam your business loan has been approved." Donna leaned back in her chair and rubbed an elbow with her hand. "Are you still planning on the festival?"

Patrick nodded. "Yes, I still want to do a grand reopening that day."

Donna smiled. "Brilliant."

Patrick didn't feel brilliant. He felt conflicted. "Tam's made it clear she's not thrilled."

"It's just business," said Donna. "This is a small town, Pat, and small towns are like family. Work things out with Tam for the Flavor Festival, and the girls will smooth things over, too. They just need a little encouragement."

"Right." He sighed. He'd come to Lagrasse for the bakery, for the children. But was that all of the truth? In the back of his mind, didn't he hope to find more than a good job and a stable home for his children? Somewhere, in the recesses of his soul, he had faith he'd find someone to love and care for him, too. Someone who would love his children as much as he did and not betray him. Donna was right. He did need to smooth things over with Piper's mother, but it could not have anything to do with his heart. Or hers.

Between Piper's drama with Scarlet, the herb shop, and a new business, Tam was overwhelmed. But life had taught her what to do about it, and Lagrasse kindly provided a way. After a couple days of nothing more than stiff nods to Patrick across the street when she saw him outside, she called the squad on Friday night to help her with the tearoom the next day. It didn't seem right to ask the bakery owner to help her, especially if their daughters couldn't get along.

Her friends came through. Saturday morning, Ali came in with Alice to watch the register at The Gracious Earth, and Kylee Hollister arrived in old clothes and toting her favorite paint brushes. The contractor had accomplished a lot. He'd finally cut a hole between the two stores, and Tam now had access from behind the shelving units in the herb shop into Petals and Pie. The new service counter was wrapped in a faux stone that complemented the dark polished floors and yellow paint. The back had a kitchen slowly being put together by a different contractor, who was in little hurry although the Flavor Festival was looming.

After giving Ali some information about which vitamins were on sale, Tam joined Piper and Kylee next door to help finish the work on the remaining walls. The room was marked with strips of painter's tape where tables and chairs would be positioned. A few potted plants had already arrived, and she scooted them closer to the window to soak up sunshine.

"What do you think of the paint?" asked

Kylee, who stepped back and appraised the last coat of *Squash Blossom*.

"It looks great." Tam smiled, filled with delight. "Thanks for coming in to help."

"I'm sorry I can't stay longer. The older twins have T-ball."

"I appreciate you coming in on a weekend when you have four kids to care for."

"They're just hanging out with Evan this morning," said Kylee. "And I'm happy for the break even if it's just a couple hours. I've got a few more minutes."

"Any help is appreciated," Tam said. She examined Piper's work as Kylee gathered her things. Piper and Scarlet were not speaking. Piper had bravely moved on the past few days, but not without a little imaginary rain cloud of sadness that dampened her usually bright spirits. Tam felt it, too. She hadn't been over to the bakery, and she felt like the wind had been taken out of her sails. Not that Patrick or pie had anything to do with her momentum.

Her daughter stopped with her arm raised in the air. "Am I doing okay?"

"You're doing great."

Piper glanced at the bare wall with the sketch of the mural. "What about that accent wall? It still needs to be painted black."

"I'll do it. And it's a brown-charcoal color. I couldn't go through with the black."

"It'll look okay. But what about the mural?"

"Mmm." Tam exhaled. Perhaps the best thing was to paint over it. But it seemed like the wrong thing to do after Scarlet had put so much work in it. "Did you talk to Scarlet at all yesterday?"

"No," admitted Piper. "I can't be friends with someone like that."

"Someone like what?" Kylee inquired.

"Scarlet Butler," explained Tam. The name echoed around the empty room over the squelch of paint from their rollers squishing on the walls.

"Ah," said Kylee, who sounded like she was already in the know. She turned to Piper. "Did you know ninety percent of relationship issues are a result of miscommunication?"

"I don't think I misunderstood when she shouted in my face."

"Oh," returned Kylee. She winced.

"She was just upset," said Tam. "She needs to learn how to deal with her emotions better."

"You think?" Piper interjected.

"Yes, but…" Tam let out a weighted breath. "Look, we already talked about it. You don't have to hang out with her if you don't want to, but you do need to forgive her and act friendly when the opportunity arises."

Piper turned back to painting with a grumble. Tam knew she missed her new friend. They liked the same music and TV shows. They both liked to read. It'd been a great start after the initial reluctance, but Piper was hyperfocused on friends and grades while Scarlet seemed hyperfocused on surviving.

"I don't blame her, you know," Tam murmured to Kylee as they rolled the paint side by side. "She's just a young girl."

"Yes, and she felt betrayed. By a friend."

"I've felt that. From a friend and a…" Tam stopped. "Well, Piper's dad anyway. And Eric. It's heartbreaking and infuriating at the same time. I don't think she meant to do it or even planned on it. She just saw Piper and—"

"Popped," said Kylee with a wink. "We all have our moments. I haven't met her, but her dad seems like a stand-up guy."

Tam took a breath. He was a good father, but… "He is," she admitted.

"We should get together," Kylee suggested.

Ali wandered in just in time to hear her, leaving the plastic sheeting between the two rooms open so she could keep an eye on the herb shop. She sat down on the floor and stirred the paint can for them. "We should get together before summer gets too busy, and we all get distracted with family plans."

Tam smiled. "That'd be nice. I'm not sure

when I'll have the time with getting the tea-room ready but—"

"You need a break," said Ali.

"I second that," said Kylee. "Burnout is not pretty." She said it as if she knew.

Tam chuckled. "I can burn out after I get the tearoom up and running."

"You're going to make it," Ali assured her. "The furniture will be in anytime. One afternoon relaxing will not kill you."

Someone rapped on the front door, and Ali jumped to her feet. Tam continued painting the last wall with the brown-black paint she'd opened, stopping her brush several inches away from the mural. Was she overreacting? Could she paint the mural herself?

"Hey," said Kylee loudly. Tam turned, noting Piper had frozen in place as Scarlet and her dad walked in.

"Hi, Ali. Nice to see you again," said Patrick pleasantly.

Tam's stomach did a cartwheel. He hadn't been around since finding out she'd known about the graffiti. She thought he was being overly sensitive about it, as if she'd purposely withheld information. She hadn't. He'd had so much going on she thought a few hints to Scarlet herself would take care of it.

Scarlet was wearing a dark blue T-shirt and

a pair of overalls. She looked nervous, and it pulled on Tam's heartstrings. Pale, the girl squeezed her fists at her side.

"Hey, Tam," said Patrick in a neighborly tone.

She turned back to the wall. "How are you?" she asked, keeping her voice level.

"We're okay. Scarlet's going to help me at the bakery today. I'm going to show her how to decorate cupcakes."

"Cool," blurted Piper, then caught herself. She glanced at Tam, then raised a paintbrush. "Hey," she said meekly to the girl across the room.

Scarlet nodded at her. "What's up?"

"Just helping my mom."

An awkward silence fell over the room. Patrick cleared his throat. "We didn't want to bother you, but Scarlet wanted to come over and see Piper," he hinted. Tam drew in a breath, realizing it was full of hope. She stopped what she was doing and turned around. Piper stared in surprise.

Scarlet gulped. "So I thought you told on me," she began, "and I lost my temper. I'm sorry." The apples of her cheeks splotched pink and red. "I shouldn't have, no matter what, but it just really hurt my feelings."

"I didn't," said Piper. Her eyes brimmed with tears. "I would have told the truth if they asked me, but no one did."

"It was someone else who wandered in that told on you," said Patrick. He looked at Scarlet severely. "Not that they were wrong."

"I know." Her voice deepened, and she stared at the floor. "I'm just used to doodling wherever and I... I didn't think about it."

Tam's heart warmed. She'd been too quick to judge the girl. Everyone had their moments. Scarlet had a lot to learn, but the most important thing she needed to know was that she was loved and accepted. Tam set down the roller on the floor. "We all make mistakes," she said, crossing the room. She reached out and touched Scarlet's shoulder. "It's normal at your age to act before thinking. That's what growing up is all about. Figuring it out."

She felt Patrick's gaze right before he said, "And you never quite get it all figured out. I've been around awhile, and I'm still learning." He glanced at Tam, and her heart betrayed her by taking flight.

She smiled. "Me, too."

He dropped his chin in an apologetic gesture. "I owe you an apology. I know you didn't intentionally not mention it."

"I really didn't think about it." Tam gave him a serious look. "And dads don't need to know every little thing."

He looked at her in astonishment. "Just the important stuff," she hedged.

"That's what friends are for." Piper smiled.

Tam gave her a teasing look. "And moms."

Patrick's and Scarlet's expressions dropped, and Tam's heart flinched. The girl's mother was no longer in her life. "I meant…" she began.

"It's okay," Patrick said quickly, but Scarlet looked hurt.

Tam walked over to her but refrained from overwhelming her with an embrace. "Scarlet, I call my mom once a week. When I have things I'm not comfortable talking to her about, sometimes I call my next-door neighbor I grew up around. In some ways, we're closer. Because you see, not all moms give life. But they nurture it."

Scarlet raised her chin as if she understood, but her expression said she had no idea how it applied to her.

Tam exhaled. "What I'm saying is, blood is family, but not all family is blood. Sometimes they're heart. And heart to heart, those are the relationships that can mean the most. Do you understand?"

Scarlet mumbled, "I think so."

"Good," said Tam. "You can't choose family, but you can choose heart." She glanced back at the wall with the blank space, thankful she'd been prompted not to paint over the sketch. Now she knew why. Scarlet didn't just need a father in her life, she needed a mother. Women. Good, strong, godly women. Tam hardly fit the bill but she tried, and she had plenty of room in her heart to mother another young woman.

"So when do you think you'll have time to paint the mural?" she asked. "The grand opening is less than three weeks away, and I have furniture and decor to deal with on top of making my teas."

The girl looked surprised, and Piper gave a happy laugh. "It wouldn't look right without it!"

"I have to help clean the school for three weeks starting next Saturday, and my dad said you changed your mind," said Scarlet.

"I jumped to conclusions, too," said Tam. "And decisions. I think this is something you need to do, and I know it's what the store needs." Patrick gave her a look of gratitude that sent her heart skipping.

A shy smile stretched across Scarlet's face. "Well, I have to help my dad first, with cupcakes and Jax. Ms. Gretchen has him right now but can't stay long."

Ali wandered back into the room with Alice at her heels. "Alice and I are going to the park in a few minutes," she said as if she'd overheard the conversation. "I'd be happy to take Jax." She looked at Patrick. "Alice will enjoy it and so will I. Her dad and brother are out fishing today."

"Thanks," said Patrick. "I can pay you. I've been looking for someone, and I've budgeted that in."

"Not today." Ali smiled. "But we should talk."

He nodded, then turned back to Tam. "I guess we'll see you later." Something warm in his eyes made her insides whir like clock gears. The olive branch meant more to her than she could say, and it gave her a strange wish for something that she knew she couldn't have. "Okay, later." She turned to Scarlet. "You can come by anytime this afternoon," she said. "This paint should be dry in a couple hours."

Excitement flashed in Scarlet's eyes, lighting her face. "Okay."

"Do you have any idea how beautiful you are when you smile?" Tam asked.

Scarlet gave a low laugh tinged with disbelief and scuttled out the door. Tam watched Patrick follow, broad shoulders pulling his shirt snug across his back. He glanced at her on his way out, and the small smile he offered just barely raised the corners of his mouth. It made the whirring become a humming, and she had to catch her breath.

Chapter Ten

Patrick's heart cracked a little when he handed Jax to Ali later, but there were four dozen cupcakes to frost, and Scarlet seemed eager to help. He was shocked she'd accepted his offer to learn, especially when he'd insisted she visit Piper and apologize.

Tam's welcome had surprised him, too. Especially after he'd accused her of withholding information. That'd been wrong. It was something his ex would have done, and he'd let the old memories ricochet off the situation. Tam's kindness toward Scarlet made him want to weep, and her quiet glances made him wonder if they could really get along. There was definitely an energy between them, something complementary, like cherry and chocolate. He chuckled to himself.

"What?" Scarlet stood at the mixer pouring in her choice of food dye, a rather shocking shade of purple.

"Er, um, nothing. I was just thinking of what flavors go together."

"Oh, I wasn't flavoring it," said Scarlet. She looked up at the extracts on the overhead shelf with interest. "Should I?"

"It's your choice. Otherwise, it's buttercream." He wondered what she was planning on doing with the purple icing and cringed as his mind pictured graffiti then bats.

Scarlet smoothed back her hair that she'd pulled into a ponytail as she examined the shelf. "I was thinking we could make pansies if you showed me how. You know, like the ones Ms. Donna has on her porch. They have little faces." She stopped as if being too cute.

Patrick smiled. "Pansies would look great. How about yellow ones, too?"

"Yes!" she said with enthusiasm. "We could do grape and banana."

Patrick laughed. "That'd be different."

She made a face. "No. How about blueberry and lemon like that pound cake you make?"

"Now you're thinking." Patrick hurried over to show her the instructions on the back of the extract bottles and how to work the math. Within minutes, they had the icings on the counter with the cooled cupcakes coated in white frosting. Patrick used a pastry practice board and showed her how to copy the outline of a flower similar to pansies. Afterward, he took a toothpick and added a few details which made her grin.

"It's just like art, but with sugar," she said, beaming.

"Exactly." Patrick grinned at her enthusiasm. "We're not so different after all," he told her. "We just use different mediums." She smiled and looked away.

After she had the hang of it, Scarlet carefully frosted her first cupcake with two purple and one yellow pansy each. It was rather good for a first try. "You got it," said Patrick. "Set that one aside, and you can eat it later as the practice piece."

"Okay." She grinned. "I haven't had cake since...well, since before I saw you again." She fell silent for a pause. "I mean it's been a long time."

Patrick patted his stomach that was in want of a few more crunches and sit-ups. "I try to keep the taste tests to a minimum, but there's nothing like a cupcake to put a skip in your step."

"Sugar does that," she deadpanned. Scarlet went back to decorating as the front door chimed. Patrick hurried to the front to serve a stream of customers. He sold five pies, two loaves of bread, and a small pound cake. Familiar faces were becoming friends. Besides Kylee, who regularly came in for sourdough, there was her husband, Evan, and his coworkers from the firehouse; Angie and Monk Coles, who were retired and went to Donna's church; and also Mrs. Lovell and a crowd of senior lady friends from the same congregation. They clearly loved muffins. After the last person left, he took a call from a Realtor about a duplex three blocks from the bank and less than a mile from the bakery. He made a note of the affordable rent, then went to check on Scarlet just as Ali Hargrove breezed in with Jax.

"I'm going to head back home now. Thought I'd drop this big boy off."

"Thank you for keeping him."

"No problem. I was playing with Alice and hanging out with the girls anyway."

"I hope he didn't get into the paint."

"No, not at all. We ended up staying next door most of the time because the park was crowded. He likes Tam's braided rug in The Gracious Earth."

"Well, it helped. Scarlet got her lesson."

Ali smiled. "I used to keep Kylee Hollister's older twins, and I help with her babies now if she needs me, so if you decide you're interested in childcare, I've been doing it on the side since Alice was born. She needs playmates, and I enjoy the company."

"What about your honey business?"

"We work with the bees on the weekends," Ali explained. "My apiary is fenced off. I have a big garden, and the kids enjoy playing outside while I weed if they're there in the mornings. I get a lot of things done in my kitchen during rest time."

It was tempting, Patrick had to admit. If this week's episode with Scarlet had taught him anything, it was that he needed help and needed to trust people beyond Donna. "You come highly recommended. Maybe I can come by sometime."

"Great idea." She grinned. "Kylee and I decided we needed to have a get-together before summer gets too crazy, and I have a little more room than she does. Why don't you join us for a barbecue? Evan is a master griller, and Tam and Gretchen and her family are coming, too."

The thought that Gretchen and Rollie would be there eased Patrick's mind, although his heart perked up at the mention of Tam's name. "I'd like that. Thanks. I know Captain Hollister. When were you thinking?"

"This weekend," said Ali. "Probably about three in the afternoon, since most of us have business, Kylee's hubby's on call, and some of the littles have sports in the morning."

Patrick gave Jax a squeeze as the baby twisted around and tried to stick his fingers in Patrick's mouth. He gave him a straw to keep him busy. "We'll be there. I think Scarlet will like that."

Patrick heard a soft intake of breath as Ali's gaze darted past him.

"What?" Scarlet whispered. The tray in her hands was poised in the air, filled with a dozen cupcakes decorated with pansies. She'd even added a silver bead in the center of each one. They looked professional.

"We were just talking about a cookout, and wow, those are fancy!" exclaimed Ali. "Do you have a wedding coming up?"

"Oh, no. Those are Scarlet's lesson for today," Patrick explained with pride.

"You just learned that today?" Ali exclaimed. "You're brilliant."

Scarlet blushed. "Thanks." Jax reached for a cupcake, and she took a step out of reach. Patrick laughed.

"Well," said Ali, dusting off her hands as if Jax had been covered with sugar. "Donna said business has picked up, so that's great since you're ready to sign the papers."

"Yes." Patrick nodded. He glanced at Scarlet. "Now we just need to find a home."

"There's plenty of land outside of Lagrasse," Ali reminded him.

"I think Scarlet likes being where the action is," said Patrick. "I may have found something here in town."

"That's understandable." Ali chuckled. "Not that there's a lot of action in Lagrasse, but we're growing."

"I'm joining the Art Club," Scarlet blurted. "They do an exhibit at the town hall once a month." She stopped as if embarrassed.

"That's right," mused Ali. "They choose a student from the middle or high school and show their work."

"I didn't know that," said Patrick in surprise. Scarlet nodded.

"Well, I better run," said Ali. "See you next Saturday if not before."

"Sure. Let me know what I can bring."

"Anything from here!" Ali laughed as she sailed out the door. "Oh, and Scarlet, Tam said she's out of the way if you want to come over and start on the mural." She waved and disappeared with Alice skipping behind her.

Scarlet put the cupcakes down on the counter and looked up at Patrick. "Can I go?"

"Of course," said Patrick. "And good job on these. They'll sell fast."

"You're going to sell them?" She sounded incredulous.

"I can't eat them all," Patrick laughed.

Scarlet's face shone with a flash of gold in her brown eyes. Her expression reminded him of a happy, pleased little girl—the one she'd never been. "I didn't think they were that good," she whispered.

Patrick shifted Jax onto his other shoulder.

"They're that good. And so are you. Go knock it out of the park on the mural across the street." She grinned. "But not too good," he warned as she collected her small backpack from underneath the counter. "We have a bakery to make number one south of Atlanta, and I'm going to need all of your skills if we're going to compete with that new tearoom across the street."

Scarlet floated blissfully out the door. Patrick felt the same way. The day had worked out—the apology, the baking lesson, and even possible childcare for Jax. He nodded at a man in baggy jeans and a striped shirt perusing the hand pies and batch of strawberry crème cannoli he'd put together the day before. "I'll be right back," Patrick assured him. He hurried to the back for the baby carrier and strapped Jax to his back. "What can I get for you?" he asked when he returned.

The man was at the register still examining the room through gold-rimmed glasses. "I hear you're buying this place."

"That's right," said Patrick.

"Quite the story. You're Donna's nephew?"

"Well, no," he admitted. "I'm a family friend. But she's like an aunt to me."

"I see." The stranger looked him up and down. "Are you Italian? Just asking because I saw the cannoli over there." He hooked a thumb over his shoulder.

Patrick smiled. "My grandparents were from Italy."

"Ah!" The man pushed glasses up on his nose, then held out a hand. "I'm Denny Flanders. I write for the county magazine."

"*County Lines?* I've seen it."

"Yes, that's it." The gentleman pointed toward the door. "Like the free ones over there." He pointed at a small table by the door stacked with napkins, booklets, and local business cards. "We write about business and arts in the area. Family news and the like."

Patrick felt his heart sink. Maybe Donna selling to a newcomer wouldn't go over well. "I have years of experience baking professionally and plan to settle here with family and friends."

"Would you be interested in an interview?" Mr. Flanders asked. Patrick hesitated. "The annual summer Flavor Festival is around the corner," Mr. Flanders explained. "We'd love to highlight you and say goodbye to Ms. Donna."

All of Patrick's reservations faded. A spotlight in the county magazine would be great for business, and Donna deserved the recognition. "That'd be wonderful."

"How about Monday?" The man inclined his head.

"I can meet you at lunchtime," said Patrick. "Donna will be in for a couple hours."

"Wonderful." The man craned his head. "We don't have a coffeehouse in town these days, so how about Pizza Pies?"

"Sure, I'll meet you there."

Jax whooped in agreement, and Mr. Flanders laughed. "See you then. Now, how about a cannoli and one of those cupcakes for my wife?"

Patrick's gaze flitted across the street. Did Mr. Flanders plan to do an article on the new Petals and Pie, too? "Um, sure," he agreed, darting for the pastry cases. "On the house."

On Sunday, Tam found herself in a pew with Piper and Scarlet between her and the pastry chef who was making it difficult to concentrate on the grand opening of Petals and Pie, not to mention a sermon on Peter's enthusiasm. For a moment, just a moment, he'd believed and done the impossible—walked on water. The thought of having enough faith to believe in anything— the life to come, peace in this life, and even love—lifted her heart. Her throat tightened when she realized all she had to do right now was have faith the new business would take off.

The next morning, Loger Street smelled like bread and sugary dreams. But it wasn't coming from her shop. Glancing across the street at the bakery, she unlocked the door to The Gracious

Earth and inhaled a breath of paint that drowned out the earthy smells of the herbs.

She walked to the doorway between the two stores and peeked in. The mural was a third of the way along, the rest of the walls and decor complete. Her plants were blooming. Equipment for the kitchen had been unpacked—electric tea-kettles, warmers, coffee makers, and a latte machine. The front of the bar was lined with the half-gallon glass jars with chrome lids waiting patiently for her dried leaves and flowers. It was beautiful. The only problem was most of the menu items, other than the ones from the Atlanta bakery order, had not arrived. She sighed at the tape lines still on the floor. Behind the store in the alley, a delivery service had dropped off enormous amounts of crates made of plywood containing her furniture. They were heavy, and some of the pieces would need to be assembled. Suddenly, overwhelmed with gratitude for her cousin, she texted Ali.

They're here.

I'll bring Heath right over.

It's a mountain of wood. I owe you for this.

You sell my honey.

We need to reconfigure the split this month.

We'll talk.

Tam knew it'd be worth it to have someone help her put the furniture together. She glanced at the mural again. It was amazing that Scarlet was only twelve. Tam could have hung framed art, but she cared deeply about Scarlet and wanted what was best for her. It was the right thing to do to help Patrick, too. She cared about him, as well, but…perhaps in a different way. Too bad they could never be more than friendly with daughters and businesses between them, but at least they could get along. The lingering problem was every time he walked in the room the scents of his laundry soap and bakery that clung to him gave her butterflies like she was a teenager who'd never had her heart broken.

She shook her head. Patrick thought he was the only one who'd been betrayed. He was as guilty as she was of throwing all of herself into her child and career. With a heavy exhale, she got to work dragging in what boxes she could move until Ali and her husband arrived. "That was quick."

"Alice is with Kylee," Ali informed her.

"You guys. Thanks for coming."

"I'm in between classes," Heath admitted. He glanced at the mural. "That's nice."

"Thanks. Piper's friend did it."

"I've heard about her," he said. He stuck his hands in his pockets and smiled. "Let's get started. What do you want me to bring in first?"

"How about you start assembling things," she suggested. "Ali and I can drag stuff in."

"No, problem." Heath held up a toolbox. "Repairs and assembly are a part of my repertoire. Just don't ask me to cut the grass."

She laughed. So did Ali. "Or smoke the bees. But you've come a long way." She pinched her husband's cheek.

Together, they got to work, Tam stopping only to check out a customer next door. Her peach tea made from Patrick's gifted canned peaches was flying out the door and so was *Strawberry Strut*. She rang up Mrs. Lovell, only to return to the group and find Heath had left. Ali was on the floor with a screwdriver and instruction book. "We've been abandoned," she laughed. "I don't mind. Hope you don't mind listening to me chatter."

"Everything okay?" Tam sat down beside her.

Ali nodded as if to herself. "Sure. I was just planning the cookout this weekend. Heath always gets uneasy with the apiary on the property."

"I'm not worried." Tam shrugged as thoughts

of Jax came to mind. "The littlest guy there will be Patrick's baby, but he's not walking yet."

"Then that shouldn't be a problem," said Ali. "Kylee's younger set of twins are walking, but they aren't as busy as their older siblings were."

Tam grinned. "What do you do when you're babysitting?"

"Lock the house down like a fort. If I take them outside, I'm right beside them. The fence around the apiary helps."

"Poor Heath," observed Tam. "He's come a long way with the bees since he first met you."

"He can't bear the thought of anyone getting swarmed like he did when he was little."

"How many stings was it?"

"About two hundred."

"I can't imagine." Tam winced.

"Like you said, he's come a long way. There's really no way to get through life without getting hurt." Ali gave her a sideways glance, then went back to turning a screw into a table leg.

"What?" Tam pressed.

Her cousin rolled her eyes.

"I'm not afraid of getting hurt," Tam protested.

Ali dropped the screwdriver and sat back on her hands. "Are you sure? I mean, not every hurt makes us run. Sometimes we fill in the fear with…other things."

"Like?" Tam arched a brow.

Ali motioned around the room.

"A tearoom? This is my business, and it's a risky venture just like the herb shop was."

"So…" said Ali, avoiding eye contact. "You'll take risks with your pocketbook but not with your heart?"

"What's my heart got to do with this?" Tam tried to feign obliviousness, but her rapidly beating pulse said otherwise. "I need college money."

"Look, you're like a sister to me so I'm just going to say it."

"Fine." Tam widened her eyes with innocent expectation, but she knew what was coming.

"Piper is the center of your universe as she should be—a part of it anyway—and the herb shop was just an avenue to providing for yourself. And this tearoom I know, is going to help you cover college tuition, but are you sure it's not a substitute?"

"Substitute for what?"

"What are you going to do when Piper leaves for school or moves away for a job someday?" Ali inquired.

Tam pulled back, stung. "I'll work."

Ali stared.

"I'll get a dog," she stammered. Not a cat. Anything but cats. Another reason to stop sneaking peeps and feeling all fuzzy and bubbly every time she looked into Patrick's eyes. He adored them.

"So a dog and two businesses."

"And you," joked Tam. But Ali was serious this time.

"It's been years since Eric moved to Chicago. Don't you think it's time to invest in someone outside of your usual circles? Make a close friend. Find someone to do grown-up things with on the weekends."

"I do grown-up things," muttered Tam.

"You work and you spend time with your daughter."

"Those are essential things."

"There are other essential things."

Tam frowned. "I think I've proven I don't need a man in my life to be happy, if that's what you're implying."

"And you're still proving it," said Ali. "You don't have to be the poster child."

"What's that supposed to mean?"

Ali searched her eyes as if she could see through them into Tam's soul. "Patrick is a good person, a great father, and if you haven't noticed, a kind, generous gentleman. He obviously wants Scarlet and Piper to be friends, and he's fond of you."

"Fond?"

"Well, he seems to enjoy your company."

"He enjoys my advice and help with his kids. And yes, he does share his peach pies."

"And?"

"What?"

Ali gave an exasperated groan. "The steady visits? Favors? The way his face lights up when you're around? He certainly was quick to make amends."

Tam forced a laugh. "He's a single dad taking over the most popular bakery in town and my main competitor on this block. Not to mention, his daughter needs a lot of help."

"Don't we all," mused Ali. She sighed. "It was just a suggestion. How about Chase Anderson?"

"Evan's friend from the firehouse?" If she had been drinking anything at the moment, it would have shot out her nose. Tam chortled. "I'm not the least bit interested in feeling out a relationship with someone who checks his hair in the mirror more than I do." She climbed to her feet. "Seriously, Ali, I'm not concerned about falling in love with anyone other than my daughter."

"Because you could get hurt again."

The truth hurt like a piano crashed onto her head. Tam frowned and walked across the room to stare at Scarlet's beautiful work. Is this what the tearoom was really about? Did she really need a second business to save enough money for Piper's future? Or was she using it to fill a void she was afraid might yawn open when her daughter started high school and became more independent?

Tam stared at the sketch of Scarlet's fountain spraying bubbles and mist. She'd found excuses for the last few men who had asked her out to dinner until they caught the drift. She was a great friend, but a friend only. The friend zone was where she shone—with everyone. She was too busy being a business owner and mother. Her chest pinched. It was fear—an uncomfortable, heavy blanket that felt more like a wet rug every time she thought about falling in love again. Tam swallowed. She was not going to carry its weight around. She shrugged it off. "So," she said, voice wavering, "what would you like me to bring to the cookout this weekend?"

Ali caught her drift. The conversation was over as far as Tam was concerned. She'd think about it, but it didn't mean she had to *do* anything about it. Not right now. Petals and Pie needed her attention, and Piper still had some things to work out with Scarlet. Romance belonged on the back burner in her life. And if she could keep it there forever, she would.

Chapter Eleven

Memorial Day weekend, Scarlet carried the Texas sheet cake up the steps to Ali and Heath Underwood's house, while Patrick juggled a diaper bag, Jax, and a play yard up to the porch. The drive to the farmhouse after picking her up from helping clean the school for the first time had been beautiful, and he wondered what it would be like to own some acreage with a small home. He liked the idea of it if things worked out until he remembered how Scarlet's face crumpled like tinfoil when he told her they'd be leaving Miami. He'd toured the duplex on a lunch break that week but hadn't mentioned it.

At least the magazine interview had gone well. He'd met Mr. Flanders for the magazine interview at Pizza Pies on Monday. Their discussion had been casual and comfortable. Patrick had been able to share his long resume and explain his connection to Donna. Later, a photographer had dropped by at closing to take a picture of them outside the store. Donna had been delighted, squeezing Patrick's arm with a happy smile while they posed. Hopefully, the article would be positive. Patrick didn't want to let her down.

Ali met them at the front door, swinging a screen open and motioning them inside. "Come on in. We're outside in the back." They dropped off the cake on an island in an open kitchen, then followed Ali through a family room full of toys and blankets to the backyard. Admiration flooded through Patrick when he stepped outside. The lot was long and wide with several garden beds on one side and a sheltered picnic table on the other. A long fence bordered the back of the property behind a wooden castle playset complete with swings and slides, and in the far corner to the northwest were stacked boxes he knew were beehives. He listened, and it seemed like the air was humming. Summer. Freedom. Happy days.

"Wow," breathed Scarlet beside him.

"Beautiful, isn't it?" Patrick murmured.

She scanned the crowd of people they would be spending the afternoon with. "It's okay."

Piper came bouncing up from out of nowhere, Alice's hand gripped tightly in her own. "Hi!" she exclaimed.

"Hey." Scarlet smiled. Their friendship was

tender, still bruised by the outburst just before school let out.

Patrick's heart flooded with gratitude for Piper's forgiveness and her mother's understanding. He was proud of Scarlet, too. It took a lot of courage to apologize and try to repair a relationship. "How are you, Piper?" he said to her. "I see you have a shadow."

"Yes." Piper looked down at Alice and giggled. "She's my little friend." She tossed back her hair. "Do you want me to take Jax?" She let go of Alice and held out her arms.

"I want Jax," said Alice, not even twice his size.

Scarlet reached for Jax almost protectively. "I got him. We should see if he can slide."

Piper laughed. "Let's go." The two girls darted off with the baby in Scarlet's arms and Alice at their heels. The playset was covered with children. Looking around for another familiar face, Patrick readjusted the strap of the diaper bag on his shoulder and walked over to the picnic table. Several adults in lawn chairs sat around chatting and laughing. There was a huge grill several feet away facing the house.

"Come on!" Ali waved him over, and beside her, Tam turned to look and smiled when she saw him. Slight tension in his back relaxed, and

Patrick found a chair and dropped the play yard and diaper bag into the grass.

Gretchen's husband, Rollie, leaned over from a few feet away and offered a hand. "How's it going, Pat?"

Patrick reached for it and gave a quick shake. "We're good. How's the construction business?"

Round and muscly, Rollie grinned. "Better. Lagrasse is growing, and with the warm weather now it's peak season." His bristly hair was shorn, and his blue eyes glowed in his sunburned face.

"I bet you're happy to have Gretchen home more often."

Rollie nodded. "Yes, it was time. And you were the first choice to replace her before they decided to sell. We're glad you're here now that Donna needs to retire. It was breaking her heart, thinking that the bakery would be closed for good."

"Thanks."

Ali bounced up with her hand looped through the arm of a pencil-slim man. He was blond, wearing a pair of tortoiseshell glasses. "Patrick, this is my husband, Heath." A black-and-white border collie squeezed up between them and gave Patrick's knees a sniff. She chuckled. "And this is Trooper."

"Hi," said Heath. "I'm glad you could make it."

"It's nice to meet you," replied Patrick. "Heard a lot about you."

Heath's mouth quirked at the corner. "Don't believe everything you hear."

Patrick laughed. "You're an accountant?"

"Yes." Heath nodded, glancing back at the steaming grill. "I also teach at the college."

"Good to know. You come highly recommended."

Heath smiled. "If you ever want to talk, have Ali give you my number."

"I'll do that." Another barnacle in Patrick's heart crumbled away. He needed an accountant, and God had put one in his path. He glanced across the shade of the shelter and met Tam's forget-me-not blue eyes. She was watching him, her fair skin dewy in the warm afternoon and hair pulled back in a petite ponytail. Did she have something to do with this? Had she helped plan a casual get-together with friends so he could get to know more people, find more branches, to reach out to his daughter? And leaves and branches eventually led to roots. She truly was the kindest woman when she wasn't so bullheaded about business and pastries. Her ebullient personality shined with sincerity and authenticity. He could see himself taking long walks with her in earnest conversation. She was a good listener and always had something interesting to say.

He gazed across the beautiful Georgia landscape. An inner warmth flooded through him, and it had nothing to do with the weather. A man in a blue baseball T-shirt that said Lagrasse Firehouse caught his attention and strolled over, and Patrick smiled in gratitude at the interruption. He shouldn't let his mind wander to the edge of such fanciful dreams.

"Hey."

Patrick rose to his feet. "Captain Hollister."

"Evan, please."

"It's nice to see you here."

He motioned toward the children crawling all over the playset. "I had to come help with the crowd control. Four of those are mine and Kylee's."

"Wow," Patrick exclaimed, trying to imagine the level of commitment.

Evan grinned. "Well, the two are adopted, her niece and nephew, and the toddlers in matching blue shirts are just over a year old."

"I don't know how she does it," Patrick exclaimed.

"Me either, but it's fun."

The man's enthusiasm for his family almost pricked Patrick's eyes with tears. He pointed. "My daughter, Scarlet, is over there with Piper. You know Jax."

"Yes, a bakery favorite."

Patrick laughed. "Ali has offered to babysit when I'm ready to look into that."

"She's great," Evan assured him. He glanced at the grill. "I better get back over and help Heath out. I told him I'd do the cooking."

"Sure, need any help?"

"No, I think we're good. Just relax." Evan pointed at a chunky cooler large enough to hold an iceberg. "Grab yourself a water or soda."

"Thanks." Patrick offered him a smile as Rollie stood up beside him. "Let's try our hand at horseshoes, Pat," he suggested. "You and me against the ladies."

Kylee shooed them away from the other side of the table. "Ya'll go ahead. I'll help with the kids on the play fort. Ali's inside."

"Does she need help?" asked Tam.

Patrick squeezed his hands into his pockets. He was hoping she would play.

"No, she insisted we relax," said Gretchen. "And I don't want to get in her way."

"Okay," said Tam with a dramatic sigh.

Patrick couldn't resist. "You don't like playing horseshoes?"

She arched a feathered brow. "I'm a little competitive."

He almost laughed, but the hint was obvious. He gave her a serious nod. "Let's go."

They lined up on either side of the two stakes

near the garden, and Patrick was surprised when Rollie and he didn't leave the ladies in the dust. The score bounced back and forth, and Tam jumped in exhilaration after every point, slapping her hands together in frustration when she missed. Her antics made Patrick laugh. He even had to ignore her playful taunts when it was his turn.

"That makes a win," he called, throwing his hands in the air on the last play of the game. Rollie laughed and whooped. "We're the champs!"

Gretchen stuck out her tongue. "You have better eyesight," she complained.

Tam huffed, then put her hands on her hips with a smile. "Congratulations, boys, you got lucky."

Patrick guffawed as Rollie chased his wife back to the awning. He met Tam in the middle of the lawn. "Lucky?" he repeated. "I happen to have years of horseshoes and bocce ball experience."

"You've spent a lot more time on the beaches than me," she pointed out. "And besides, it was by one point. Come on, that was luck."

"Maybe," he relented. "But all that matters in the end is the final score."

"Right," she said with a wry laugh. She squinted at him as they walked back to the awning. The smell of grilling hamburgers and hotdogs filled the air, chasing away the fragrance of tilled earth and blossoms. "I think you need to admit you're a little competitive, too."

She was taking it a lot harder than he would have. He gave her a playful nudge with his elbow. "Would you rather I had let you win? Not made you try?"

"No," she said quickly and then she relented with a smile. "No, I like being motivated. Fair is fair. It's just I was thinking of…well, I have a lot on my mind."

"Like the grand opening?"

"Yes, the Flavor Festival."

"It's going to be fine," Patrick assured her. Was she worried about losing business to him during the event? "I promise not to stand on your side of the street and redirect traffic to the bakery."

She laughed. "It's not just that. Everything's about ready, but I'm still waiting on the bulk order of the menu items from the EU. I guess I'll have to make do."

"Oh. I see." An idea popped into Patrick's mind, interrupted by Ali, who dashed by with a bucket full of an array of condiments. No. Tam would never order menu items from him.

"Need help?" Tam offered Ali. She pulled her hair up to wipe her damp neck, showing off fair and dainty earlobes.

"Yes, can you run in and bring the chips and buns out?"

"Sure."

"And desserts!" Ali called as she hurried to the picnic table.

"I'll help," Patrick told Tam. He followed her to the house, appreciating her figure as she glided up the back porch steps. They reached the kitchen island together, and Patrick stopped short of asking her where she got all the energy to be there for everyone.

"Are you okay?"

"I'm fine," he murmured. She was an amazing woman.

"You said you had an idea about the menu items?" Tam stacked bags of hamburger and hot dog buns in her arms.

"Oh, yeah." Patrick peeled the lid off the sheet cake and gathered his thoughts, thankful for the distraction. Business—for their daughters' sake. But he wanted a slice of cake to fill the sinkhole opening up in his chest. To patch the ruins of his scarred heart. It couldn't be done with Tam, so he had to quit considering it. "I just wanted to make a suggestion."

"What's that?" She stepped closer to listen, arms bobbling under her burden of bread and the bags of chips in her free fingers.

Patrick admired the way her lashes curled

against her light skin and framed her eyes. They were portraits of beauty. "I—uh, well, I was going to suggest you just order goods from the bakery."

"The Last Re-Torte?"

"Yes. What other bakery is there?"

Tam shifted her jaw as if thinking. He held up a hand. "I know you have your grand opening for the Flavor Festival. So do I. But rather than competing, why don't we work together?"

"You want me to sell your pies in my shop thirty feet across the street from you?"

He nodded. "And I could carry a couple of your teas."

"That doesn't make sense."

"Why not? If they like your tea at my place they'll come over and buy a bag. And if you offer a few of my pastries, they'll swing by the bakery for more."

Tam gave him a steady stare. "How about you make something exclusive for my shop," she suggested. "And I keep my teas."

"Like?"

"Scones?"

"I can provide scones."

"English and traditional?" she challenged him.

"I've baked all kinds of international delicacies," he assured her. "I can make a scone. But may I suggest you give it local flair? That's what the tearoom is about now, isn't it? Spotlighting local?"

"Like peaches?" She arched a brow and looked so cute he felt his mouth stretch into a smile.

"Peaches, absolutely," he murmured, although he'd meant blueberries.

Tam stilled, and he worried she could hear his galloping heartbeat. Suddenly, he wanted to feel hers. He would have dropped the cake if he was holding it. Patrick stepped into her, his mouth working to say something, anything, to put together the ingredients of what he was thinking and feeling. She did not move back or look away, and in that split second he was both shocked and delighted. Blue eyes locked onto his, and he was sure he saw notes of lavender. The bread bags in Tam's arms made a soft sound when they hit the floor, and it was the last thing Patrick heard, because she met him halfway, lashes dropping shut and long fingers reaching up to cup his jaw as their lips met in a slow, tender kiss.

The day after Memorial Day, Tam unlocked Petals and Pie and strolled in with a searching gaze. The paint had dried, and the mural was halfway finished. Everything was about ready, minus the menu, but she and Patrick had come to an agreement. He'd brought Scarlet over following the picnic on Saturday after dropping

Jax off with Donna, and they'd talked through a compromise while watching her paint late into the evening with Piper as chaperone. Neither girl knew that their parents had shared a kiss that almost crushed the hamburger and hot dog buns. A pounding of footfalls up the back porch steps had interrupted them, and Patrick had grappled with the bags on the floor to help Tam pick them up just as Ali burst through the door out of breath. Tam had disappeared so fast she was sure he never saw her leave, and she kept her distance from him until the girls blindsided them with the request to go over to the tearoom and paint later.

Tam almost broke out in hives when she thought about them catching her and Patrick in the act. Silly, foolish. It was a mistake and might make things weird between the girls. Worse, it could make things weird between her and Patrick when they already had two grand openings on the same day. Tam took a deep breath and examined her new furniture. The dining benches and chairs were beautiful. The shop would be a success, she was sure of it. And all because of Piper's and Scarlet's ideas. Proof, she realized, that children, and especially young adults, deserved to be heard.

Patrick and she had formed a partnership now, a quid pro quo between the stores, and she couldn't mess it up. She sighed and sank down into a chair looking across the street. It didn't help that it was the sweetest, most tender kiss she could remember. She flushed when she thought about how she'd dropped the things she'd been holding.

Patrick must have though she had no reserve. He had no idea he's swept her heart into the atmosphere for moments that felt much longer than a few seconds. And the look he'd given her when they'd parted after Ali rushed into the room had made her forget to breathe for half a minute. It'd been more than charm or flirtation. It held an offering and suggested there was hope—which made no sense. Even if she dared consider something with someone again, well, it couldn't be Patrick. She exhaled, then jumped when someone rapped on the door.

Heat flooded through her cheeks when she saw it was him. Had he seen her reminiscing? Did he know? She'd forced herself to get back to business on Saturday night, and on Sunday made sure to be a few minutes late so the girls didn't put them all together in a pew again. But she did wave when she left the sanctuary after hurrying Piper along. The girls could call or text later. She'd planned to talk business with Patrick on Monday, and here he was.

He raised a hand, giving her a meek wave.

Tam pushed away the regrets and pulled up a smile. She pushed the door open, meeting his examination for just a fleeting moment. "Good morning."

"Morning." Patrick walked in wearing a pair of fitted slacks and his usual white shirt, arms olive and tan. He smelled soapy and fresh, which seemed too familiar. She assumed he hadn't started baking yet. "How's the mural?"

Tam pointed at the finished painted fountain and its greenery. "It dried fine and just a few of the people in the background are left to finish. And the border."

He folded his arms and put a hand to his chin. "Do you like it?"

"I think it's sweet, captures Lagrasse, and invites you to relax like you're at home."

"Home. I think you're right." He cleared his throat. "I just wanted to give you a heads-up that I'm going to email you four scone recipe suggestions to choose from."

"Great," said Tam, realizing he was all business, too. But she was intimately aware that they were alone again. "Where's Jax?"

"Scarlet has him this morning. Donna will bring him over to the bank after lunch."

"You're signing the papers for the bakery."

"Yes, and just in time."

A pinch nipped her chest, but Tam brushed

it away. She knew it was coming. "Congratulations," she said, and she meant it. "Thanks for offering to sell me the scones. I'm sure they'll go over well if they're as good as your peach pies."

At the word, *peach*, he caught her gaze and held it. Peaches. Right. "Blueberries will be in season soon," she stammered. She ignored a building heat in her neck and took a deep breath. "Look, about Saturday," she began. The dismissal tangled in her throat, and her cheeks blazed with mortification.

As usual, Patrick had her covered. "No worries. I'm sorry if I stepped over the line. It was a moment and I… I just…"

"I got caught up in the moment, too," Tam filled in quickly to avoid an excruciating pause. "I'm sorry." She gave him a gentle smile, hoping he knew that it took everything she had in her not to admit that she'd fall over and float away if he'd do it again. "About the girls," she said, hoping the subject could be dropped. "Do you think Scarlet can come over and finish the mural soon?"

"Sure," said Patrick. "Now that school's out, she's going to help me on Tuesdays and Thursdays while Ali watches Jax. Scarlet will babysit at Donna's on other days this summer. I'm going to pay her."

"Oh, she'll like that. And I need to settle up with her over the mural."

He nodded. "She'd appreciate it. I explained the benefit of opening a bank account, and we even talked about getting some kind of debit card."

"Wow, great thinking," Tam admitted, as the awkward air between them dissipated. "I haven't even started that with Piper. I guess I do too much for her."

"She's lucky to have you," said Patrick. He cleared his throat quietly, and Tam could have sworn he was inching for the door. "I better head over and get started. Let me know which scones you're interested in and give me an estimate so I can work that into my schedule."

"No problem. And I appreciate you offering, since you have a lot of baking to do for the festival."

"Right. Well, talk at you later." He waved, and she chuckled at his use of the local expression he'd picked up.

She waved back. "I'm grabbing Piper at lunchtime, and she's going to mind the herb shop while I work in here this afternoon. She may be over for a pie."

"Send her on!" he said cheerfully and headed out the door.

Patrick darted across the street. He hurried to the ovens after nodding at Gretchen when they passed each other at the counter. She was transferring chocolate-eclairs from a tray to the glass case that housed fritters and hand pies. He shook his head to dismiss Tam from his head. Clapping his hands together, he looked around for his apron. His forearms ached to knead. No more kissing talk—or, well, kissing.

As he suspected, given the way Tam had acted the rest of the night on Saturday, and her casual greeting on Sunday, the kiss had meant nothing. It'd just been an incidental reflex, like flinching when someone brushed past you. She'd been standing there with her beautiful spirit and radiant energy, and he'd blanked on the party outside, even his children. Brushing his lips over hers had made him forget he was a pastry chef with a new business that needed his undivided attention, and she worked across the street. But she'd made it clear there was nothing deep or intimate behind the kiss, and he knew better than to risk thinking she could feel something like that for him.

After Ali's fortunate interruption, he'd carried the cake and a few bags of chips outside without turning cartwheels in front of the beekeeper. She'd gurgled on like a fountain about her to-do list and the tons of food all over the counters, oblivious to the fact he'd kissed her cousin. Patrick had swiped at his brow to dismiss the relief. He couldn't imagine what he would have done if it'd been one of the girls who'd walked in on them. He groaned quietly at his dumb luck and headed to the sink to wash his hands. A few loaves of sandwich bread would fill up the rack, and that required lots of kneading. He needed to get his head out of the clouds and as far away from Petals and Pie as possible.

Chapter Twelve

After lunch with Piper at Pizza Pies on Wednesday, Tam headed back with a satisfied appetite. Leaving her daughter at the herb shop register with a book from her summer reading list, Tam walked through the breezeway with her arms full of teas to fill up the beautiful glass canisters for Petals and Pie. The dried flowers and fruit looked so pretty through the glass that she thought she would cry. A single box from Italy had arrived during lunch, and she unpacked biscotti and stacked it prettily in chrome wire serving racks on the back counters. It wasn't much, but after she stepped back to admire it, she unpacked a box of ceramic mugs from an online order. Her change of direction for the shop meant she needed unique pieces so she was looking forward to ordering a few special cups a month from local artists who fired them in their kilns. Again, it was Scarlet who'd given her the idea. Patrick's daughter was a bright child with oodles of talent just waiting to find its way out.

And it would, as Scarlet learned to trust and love herself. She'd already begun with the mural.

Tam heard a faint happy jingle as Piper shouted, "Mom!" from the next room. Tam set down a mug and strolled over to The Gracious Earth.

A trio of women wearing large earrings and carrying purses the size of cargo containers trooped inside, and Tam gave them a wave. "Hello, ladies." The honey was in, and the store was glowing. School was out, and business was picking up as tourists came through town on summer vacation. With the sign up on the tearoom next door, the decor ready, and the small kitchen and supplies coming together, the grand opening for her second business was finally on schedule for the Flavor Festival. She just needed to get the word out.

Tam straightened a stack of the flyers for the festival and waited patiently as the women chatted and browsed. Piper picked up her book and motioned toward the tearoom, disappearing with it next door where she would probably break in one of the cozy chairs set up in a corner. One of the customers toddled up in thick cork bed sandals and grinned. "I love that you sell local honey here," she said with enthusiasm. "My grandson is a beekeeper."

"Is that so?" said Tam. "Whereabouts?"

"We're from Birmingham," drawled the woman. "On our way to Destin for a girls' weekend."

"That's exciting."

"Yes." The lady grinned. "Crafters convention, and of course, the beach." She held up a wrist that jangled with homemade bangles. One charm read, Emmajean.

"Sounds exciting."

"It will be. You look busy." The lady glanced at the doorway between the two stores.

"Petals and Pie is opening next week," Tam explained.

"Oh, a coffeehouse?" said Emmajean.

"Tearoom actually," said Tam. "Healthy herbal drinks and smoothies. And pie."

"Oh? Do you own both?"

"I do." Tam smiled. "It seemed like a natural expansion."

"I suppose so." Her chatty customer's friend walked up beside them. "Ready to go get a muffin?"

"I am," Emmajean cried cheerily. "Good luck with your tea and pie." She stepped back as her friend plopped a bag of peach tea on the counter. "You're going to have your work cut out for you with that bakery across the street."

"Don't I know it." Tam smiled faintly.

Emmajean's friend nodded, earrings rattling.

"Oh yes, but I'm going to take a doughnut over a cup of tea anytime."

"I'll have some of their pastries here," Tam assured them.

"Will you?" said Emmajean as if confused. "It didn't mention that in the article."

"What article?"

"You know, your hometown magazine."

"The one that just came out," said Emmajean's friend. She pulled the free magazine out of her purse that the county published every month. Flipping it open to a dog-eared page, she pointed at a photo of The Last Re-Torte with a handsome, smiling Patrick standing in front of the window with his arm looped through Donna's. *Beloved Bakery Passes Into Capable Hands* read the caption.

The sun was beaming down on the bakery like a rainbow of approval. Patrick looked like the son Donna had always wanted. The windows behind them were bursting at the frames with cake stands and colorful serving trays. Tam tore her eyes away and gave the customers a tight smile. "I haven't read it yet, but that's wonderful." It'd help if Patrick looked like an ogre.

"Oh, yes," cooed the woman. "From one pastry chef to another, and he's a single dad." She wagged her head.

"Amazing," echoed Emmajean.

"Yes, amazing," Tam repeated. Patrick was amazing. But did he have to be so amazing right now?

"We'll have to come back for the Flavor Festival," said Emmajean.

Tam squared her shoulders. "I hope you do. Petals and Pie will be opening that weekend with lots of specials."

The woman with the annoying earrings rattled them again. "Oh, honey, that sounds nice." She glanced across the street. "But you got to admit, an Italian bakery is going to be a lot more exciting." She grinned and pointed at her voluptuous hips. "Let's go, Emmajean."

Tam nodded goodbye instead of protesting that it wasn't an Italian bakery as the trio left the store and skipped across the street. The festival was a week and a half away, and The Last Re-Torte had its own article in the local arts magazine. Now, she'd lost some customers.

She slapped the receipt in the till drawer and threw her arms around her waist. Petals and Pie would have art, pie, tasty and unique herbal teas, and all kinds of curious and fun imported snacks—if they arrived. She glanced around The Gracious Earth and its local products. Maybe she'd missed the mark.

She pursed her lips and frowned at the bakery across the street, then headed next door to join Piper. But it wasn't the bakery she was really upset about. Patrick had been interviewed for an article in *County Lines* and not bothered to mention it. He'd had all last weekend to do so. Instead, he'd come on as someone who cared about her daughter, her friends…and he'd had the nerve to kiss her!

After the lunch rush, Patrick raced home to check that Donna had picked up Scarlet from the school after her cleaning punishment. He spent a few minutes with them, packed up his grand reopening sign, and after tucking the baby down for a nap and encouraging Scarlet to start painting on her new canvas he'd given her, hurried back to the bakery to turn out some cinnamon roll dough and thaw fresh fruit for another round of pies. He was doubling the recipes and freezing batches. The freezer was bursting.

With a faint smile, he started folding and kneading, knowing he couldn't have done it without his new friends in Lagrasse, Donna, or his little girl. Even Jax was doing okay with the change in routine. Patrick made sure to spend as much time as possible with the kids when they were together. Especially if he was going to preach to Scarlet that cell phones ate up time and stole precious moments. He made sure to keep his intervals online to a minimum, but if he had checked the latest local news, he could have expected the visit.

The Last Re-Torte's front door chimes jingled in warning, and he dusted off his hands. Hurrying to the front, his mood ballooned even higher when he found Tam at the register. "Lunch break?"

"Already took one with Piper," she replied. Her cheerful grin was missing.

Tam was in business mode. He recognized it now. "Everything okay over there?"

"I thought it was," she said.

He leaned over the counter, glancing at the small lips he'd kissed and admiring the Cupid's bow. "What's wrong?" He was eager to help, more than he should be, but regardless of reasons he'd keep to himself, he owed her.

She pulled a rolled magazine out from under her arm and dropped it on the counter. "This. It's bothering me, and I don't want to stew, so I thought I'd ask about it now since Piper asked me to pick up a couple of hand pies."

Patrick looked down at the open magazine and saw a picture of Donna—then recognized himself. "Oh!" He picked it up and scanned the photo. The title made him beam. "I didn't know this was out."

"You knew it was coming?"

"Well, yeah, I'm in the picture."

"So you knew about the article?"

"Sure. The writer came by a couple weeks ago, and we met at the pizza place for an interview."

"It's quite in-depth. You sound interesting and exciting."

"Exciting. Me?"

"Yes, with all of the experience you're bringing with you. They even mentioned the peach pies."

Patrick heard a tinge of apprehension in Tam's voice. His forehead wrinkled. "This is bothering you?"

"Patrick, I'm opening a new business, and you're taking over a bakery that's been here for more than six years."

"So?" He tossed in a soft chuckle to drain the tension.

"You could have told me."

"I guess you're right," he said. "I thought about mentioning it, but to be honest, I kind of put it in the back of my mind."

Tam looked upset, and his stomach sank. "I wasn't keeping it from you, not like…"

"Like me not telling you about Scarlet drawing in the school restroom?"

"That didn't even cross my mind," said Patrick, frustration forming in his veins.

She studied him. "Are you sure?"

"Of course. Look, Tam," he said with an exhale. "I thought we worked this out. I'm not out to get you. I have no secret motive to get in your way."

"This is in my way because I didn't even get a mention," she admitted.

"I had nothing to do with it," Patrick promised. "In fact, I told him how helpful you and the other business owners have been. I mentioned you by name."

"Oh," she said, somewhat mollified. "Fine. I just wanted to ask about it. I felt blindsided. And then there were those ladies."

"Yes. Thanks for sending them over."

"I didn't. They saw the sign for fried pies and beelined right over here."

"Well, I hope they gave you some business, too."

"They didn't," Tam admitted. "They set down the tea and honey they were interested in and headed over because of the article."

"I'm sorry," said Patrick.

"You can't be." She cut him off. "It's business. All's fair in love and war and business and all that."

"This isn't war," said Patrick. He tripped over the words when he deleted *love* from his sentence. *No love here.* Even if he had to fight it, put the oven on broil and let whatever this was burn to ashes.

"I know," said Tam calmly. "I've always gotten along with Donna, and I want to keep things civil for the sake of the girls. This isn't horseshoes."

Patrick was confused again. It was like she was saying the article was a problem. Like it was a return volley in a battle at sea. "I count you as a good friend, a special friend, Tam." Dare he mention the kiss. No, he couldn't. Shouldn't. It needed to remain history like so much of his past. "I'll try to keep you informed."

"No, that's just it," she explained. "You're not obligated to tell me anything about the bakery. And I'm not obligated to share anything about my stores. Having the girls be such close friends is... Well, to keep things from getting muddy, I felt like I needed to say something and set a boundary."

"Oh." Suddenly the counter between them felt as wide as the ocean. "So what's the boundary?"

"Business and the girls?"

"You don't want to pal around at picnics and play horseshoes?"

"Not if it's going to end in kissing," she replied. His cheeks flushed, and his heart sank a meter or three when he realized she was nonplussed. Her smile was polite. Her opinions about what kind of friends they were going to be were obvious. Neighbors with shops across the street from each other. Business acquaintances whose daughters were friends.

"Right," he said, chest heavy. He imagined a half dozen new barnacles on it. Strong, stubborn, crusty ones that couldn't be chipped away or pried off. She was right, he knew it.

"So what did you want for Piper?" he asked, turning toward the display cases. The quicker he checked out Tam at the register, the sooner she would leave and he could go back to kneading dough, if not throwing it against the walls. The woman was all kindness and cheer unless you got in her way. Then she was a cold and stubborn fish—strong and impossible to land. But he wasn't interested in landing her, he reminded himself, as she strode out the door and headed back across the street. Or any other woman for that matter. He knew better than to ever try hooking another heartbreaker again.

Tam drove the few blocks home after closing on Wednesday with a cinder block still in her chest. The magazine article had been the talk of the town all day. Piper hummed to the radio as her common sense warred with her emotions. There were things bothering Tam more than the bakery's spotlight and popularity. It was him. Ever since Patrick set foot in Lagrasse, he'd turned her head, made her feel special, and proved that she was needed. She'd started to think about the future in a different way. Tam squeezed the steering wheel. She'd been duped twice, and no matter how friendly and charitably she treated others, it didn't mean she was owed the same by the universe.

Piper, she reminded herself. Her daughter was her purpose, her mission, her everything. There was nothing wrong with giving Piper all of her. Just because a part of her ached for a bigger family and to feel settled and secure in life, didn't mean she should expect it. With a creeping realization, Tam realized that she'd never prayed for it, because voicing it would be asking for something she might never receive. Her daughter and shops were blessings enough. She didn't deserve more. She wouldn't risk considering love ever again.

Her heart did a swan dive to the floorboard at the discussion in her head. Why was she thinking about these things and Patrick at the same time?

You did a good job. You had a concern, and you took it right over and cleared it up. All business.

Telling herself she was satisfied that everything was working out as it should, she pulled into the driveway and let herself into the house with Piper on her heels. Her daughter was eerily quiet. "Should you be on your phone so much?" Piper gave her a half frown and hurried to her room and shut the door. That wasn't like her.

Tam set her handbag and some paperwork on the kitchen counter and opened the freezer to stare inside. Her premade frozen dinners looked cold and bland, and she wasn't sure what half of them were since she didn't label leftovers consistently. She took a guess and pulled out something that looked like it would defrost quickly. Piper was still in her room. Bouncing back and forth between giving her independence or hovering, the suspicious quiet became too much, and Tam finally walked down the hall and knocked on Piper's bedroom door.

"Hey in there, is everything okay?"

After a pause, Piper said, "Yes, ma'am."

Tam cracked the door open. "Are you sure? You're awful quiet."

Piper looked up from her position on the bed. She hadn't unpacked or changed into her comfy lounging shorts. The phone was still in her hand. Tam's nerves tightened. "Piper, you know you're not supposed to be on that unless you need to contact me or someone else. Are you playing an offline game?"

Piper met her stare, her honest nature clouding her eyes. Tam waited patiently. Finally Piper said, "It's Scarlet. You said she could text me."

"Yes. Is she okay?" After a weighty pause, Tam said, "No?"

"I don't think she wants anyone to know."

"About what? Summer school suspension? Who'll find out? Everyone's out of school."

Piper glanced down at her screen again. "It's not that, Mom. It's… I'm worried, so I'm going to tell you even if she gets mad again."

"Okay."

"Scarlet's mother called today."

A jolt of surprise hardened Tam's spine. "What?"

"Yes, from jail or something."

"But how?"

"On Ms. Donna's phone."

"How did she get the number?" Tam wondered.

Piper shrugged. "I guess her dad gave it to her or somebody at her prison."

"Maybe it was a counselor or social worker," Tam said, thinking out loud. She couldn't imagine a man as kind as Patrick refusing to let his ex-wife talk to her kids.

"Mr. Butler lets Scarlet send her letters, but mostly she draws pictures. Her mother only wrote back to her one time, and she said some weird stuff like she was sorry, and she'd see her soon or something."

"It's not going to be soon, I don't think."

"That's what Scarlet said. And that's why her dad really doesn't want them talking on the phone. Even when her mom gets out, Scarlet and Jax will still live with their dad."

"That's the long-term expectation for now." Tam crossed the room and sat down on the bed, trying not to peek at the text exchange. "Is Scarlet upset?"

Her daughter stared at her phone as if considering what to share, then turned it face down in her hand. "Scarlet was alone."

"Uh-oh. What did the woman say?"

Piper's eyes suddenly filled with tears. "She told her everything was her fault. She told her if she would have kept her mouth—" Piper made air quotes "—shut, the baby wouldn't have been taken away, and she wouldn't have gotten arrested." Piper's eyes were wide as she crossed over into the reality of the adulthood that awaited her. "Mom, she said her mother drank a lot and took drugs. Weird people came into their house."

"I know." Tam wrapped an arm around her daughter's shoulder. "The ugliness in the world we've talked about is real, Piper, and Scarlet saw some of it." Tam's throat went dry at the possibilities. "Did she tell you anything else?"

"No," said Piper. "But she's crying and real upset. Her mom told her it was her dad's plan all along and that she fell for it."

"I'm so sorry." Tam shook her head. "I know that's not true. He didn't know where they were living when those things happened. It's a lot easier to blame other people for our mistakes than to face them."

"But she's her mom," Piper exclaimed.

"I know, and I don't understand it," said Tam. "I haven't walked in her mother's shoes, but it was a terrible thing to do, especially when Scarlet's beginning to heal, make friends, and settle down here."

A tear escaped from Piper's eye, and Tam gave her a warm embrace. "You're a good friend for caring so much, and you did the right thing telling me. Mr. Butler needs to know."

"B-but she got so mad last time," stammered Piper. "I don't want to tell anyone."

"You didn't have a choice because I asked you. Then I took your phone."

Piper stared in surprise. "Do you mean lie?"

Tam snatched the phone from her and waved it in the air. "Nope. I'm concerned about why you're upset, and I'm going to read these texts whether you like it or not."

Piper's mouth dropped open, and she worked her jaw but no words came out. Tam started out of the room with the phone and no protests from her daughter. "Promise me something."

"What?" said Piper.

"Scarlet may have more things she wants to talk about sometime. Worse things. If there's anything you have questions about or think I need to know, I want you to come to me. Okay?" Uncertainty flitted over her daughter's face. "Piper? Okay?" Tam insisted. "It's hard enough to handle bad things as a grown-up. Twelve going on thirteen is not old enough to understand everything. You come to me. Ask anything."

Piper's eyes brimmed over. "Okay, Mom. I'm glad I have you."

Tam smiled, her heart aching at the hole in their lives. Her daughter deserved a father, too. Just as much as Scarlet needed a mom. Handling this the right way was a cloudy issue. It'd be so nice to have someone close to bounce her thoughts off besides her own parents.

Tam headed back to the kitchen where the microwave was intermittently reminding the empty room the food was done. She dumped it out on two plates and put them back in on warming mode, then leaned against the counter to examine the texts. Her stomach shrank before simmering with anger. Patrick needed to know. Just in case his daughter didn't tell him, he needed to be informed she'd been jerked back into her old life and needed to be protected.

Chapter Thirteen

Scarlet had a headache so she stayed in her room as Patrick helped Donna pick up the kitchen after dinner. Jasmine crept around the table, and Patrick wondered why the Siamese cat wasn't with his daughter. "Was Scarlet like this when you got home?"

Donna nodded. "I left Gretchen's at three-thirty, and when I got here, Jax was crawling around the living room. She'd gated it to keep him corralled, but she was lying on the couch staring at the ceiling—very pale."

"And she said she had a headache?"

"She did. And she seems a little morose."

"I thought so, too, but that's a teenager thing, right?"

"Some of the time. Just keep an eye on it," Donna suggested.

"She has two more Saturdays of suspension at the school," said Patrick. "Maybe she's annoyed."

The doorbell rang. "I'll get that." Donna hurried out with Felix and Jasmine at her heels as if they'd get a treat from any stranger who happened to visit.

"Traitor," Patrick called to the big ginger. He wiped the orange sauce off of Jax's chin and picked up the rice the baby had flung all over the high chair tray. "You're a mess," he said, with a grin. Jax slapped the tray with this hands and looked up for approval. "How about a cookie?" Patrick suggested. Jax knew that word and made a whooping sound.

Chuckling, Patrick turned to the cookie jar. Scarlet loved cookies, too. It was clear she didn't get treats when she was little, not to mention a good dinner, so she rarely turned down either. He hadn't offered her anything for her headache, so he opened a cabinet with pain relievers and vitamins and looked for something safe. He knew what Jax needed for a fever. No idea what to do to give a teenage girl who needed relief.

"He's in here." Donna's invitation caught his attention. Patrick looked back in curiosity.

"Tam," he said, ignoring how pleased he felt to see her. *Business and boundaries.* "Did I forget something?"

"No." Her gaze darted to Jax. "I'm sorry to bother you without calling. But I thought I should come right over."

Patrick's mind raced through pastry orders,

customers, and then the magazine article. He tensed. Tam's drive was admirable, but she kept veering into his lane, all the while accusing him of doing the same thing! "This couldn't have waited?"

She glanced at him. "Okay, I deserve that." Donna gave him a look then left the room. Tam walked over and pulled a chair out beside Jax. His eyes brightened when he saw her. "Mmm, cookies," she said, then snarled like the Cookie Monster. The baby chortled. She then sneezed without warning, and chagrined, turned back to Patrick with a sniffle. "Where's Scarlet?"

"Upstairs. She has a headache." He shut the cabinet door and folded his arms, confused and filled with apprehension.

"That's why I came," said Tam. "I suspected you wouldn't know."

"Know what?"

Tam glanced toward the door as if worried someone might be listening. Patrick moved over to the table and pulled out the chair on the other side of Jax. Jasmine hopped on his lap and Tam's eyes widened.

"She's harmless. The cat, I mean. What's going on?"

"Piper got a text from her a few hours ago. Scarlet's mother called."

Patrick's chest constricted. "What? How?"

"You and Donna weren't here, and she called the house."

He exhaled to loosen his chest but a knot in his back pinched. "I gave her the number in the event of an emergency. I didn't want her to have mine, and Scarlet didn't have a phone. Not until I gave her one using the same plan you have for Piper."

"Right. Well, her mother said some pretty awful things."

His dinner turned into a hard lump in his stomach. "That's her M.O. What'd she say?"

"I think you should read it." Tam passed him her cell phone, eyeballing Jasmine and sniffled. "I took screenshots of Piper's texts."

Patrick looked at the images, and his tension turned into sharp pain. He could feel his ears getting hot and realized he was squeezing the phone like a boa constrictor gripping its food. He handed it back to Tam abruptly. "I had no idea."

"I know. And Piper felt it was serious enough to tell me, even though she's afraid of being a tattletale and making Scarlet mad again. I made her tell."

"It doesn't matter. This is important."

"I know. So throw me under the bus. Piper didn't hand me her phone. She just told me about the call and that she was concerned. I took her phone and read the messages. I'm here to tell you because I love Scarlet and want to keep her safe."

She loved her? Patrick's throat knotted. Having someone see the good in Scarlet was a relief and a blessing. It made him love, er, appreciate, Tam more. He glanced through the kitchen door. "I should go talk to her. She needs to know what her mother said is not true. This is not a backward town, I have never had it in for her, and nothing that happened was my little girl's fault."

"I can't imagine having to deal with something like this with Piper's dad. Here." Tam pulled a copy of the *County Lines* magazine out of her purse. "I brought this for you. Show it to her first. Let her be proud of you. Then ask her about the phone call."

"Good idea. And you know if I check the caller ID I'd see the number."

"That's true, but she needs honesty. She hasn't had that in her life, either."

"Okay. I'll tell her how I know. I think it's best."

"And this is my doing, not Piper's," she reminded him. "I didn't give Piper any choice."

Tam was fearless. Patrick studied the woman across the table from him. "Thank you. This means a lot."

She smiled. "Anyone else would have done the same thing."

"Take the heat?"

"I think you've spent enough time in the fire," said Tam. She looked at Jax fondly. "Do you want me to keep an eye on this guy?" She looked over her shoulder as if Jasmine might be hunting her.

He opened his mouth to say no, that Donna was there, but suddenly Patrick wanted Tam nearby. And besides, Donna had already retired to the living room, sore and exhausted like she always was at the end of the day.

"Please," he said. "Donna already helped with dinner so I know she's worn out. Jax's toys are in the living room, or he enjoys being out in the peach orchard. No cats outside."

Tam glanced past him through the picture window behind the dinner table. The sun was still in the sky, but had lost most of its luster. "We'll go for a walk," she said. "How about letting me use your piggyback contraption? And you keep the cats."

He agreed as she let out another sneeze.

Patrick's ankles felt like they had thick chains wrapped around them while he trudged up the narrow stairs to the guest room. He knocked on the door and waited in the still air. After a pause, Scarlet opened the door and stared at his feet as if she couldn't bear to look him in the face. It was impossible to miss the red rims around her eyes and the streaks down her cheeks. "Yes?" she said, her voice low and normal as if she'd just been reading a book.

"I wanted to see how you were doing." He held up the bottle of pain reliever.

"I'm fine."

"Can I come in?"

Scarlet opened the door wider and shuffled back to the bed. Patrick followed and sat down beside her. She looked at him in surprise, then darted her eyes away and wiped her palms across her cheeks.

Patrick longed to know how to approach such a volatile subject, especially with such a sensitive and scarred young girl. "Hey, so I heard from Tam a few minutes ago, and she wasn't happy."

"I didn't do anything," said Scarlet quietly.

Patrick propped a foot on the bedrail trying to act casual. "I know."

"Is she okay?" Scarlet took a deep breath tinged with mild relief.

"She is, but she's worried about you."

"Why?" Her voice was lined with dread. Still, she wouldn't meet his eyes.

Patrick wrapped his arms around his knee. "She told Piper to put her phone away, and when she didn't, she took it from her."

"Oh."

"I'd like to speak about your mom," said Patrick carefully.

"It's fine," mumbled Scarlet.

"It's not fine," he disagreed. "Will you talk about it?"

"I don't really want to. It's lame to be upset about her."

Her refusal thumped his chest. Patrick grasped for words while his heart fumbled for inspiration. "Can I tell you a story?"

Her lip quirked to the side as if she was fighting a sarcastic remark.

Patrick cleared his throat. "Once upon a time I met a girl at my after-school job my senior year of high school. She ended up quitting, but we kept hanging out. Then it got serious."

"And I came along?"

"No. She started working at a nice restaurant. I went to culinary school. But I couldn't focus because I loved her."

"You did?"

Patrick nodded. "I did. So I married her. I still had two years left, so she worked full-time while I studied and got a part-time job."

Scarlet nodded to herself as if she'd heard a version of it.

Patrick squeezed his knee. "You came along right before I graduated. And we loved you."

She looked at him doubtfully. "She didn't want me."

"She really loved waiting tables. Hanging out with her coworkers."

"I thought she was a bartender."

"She got into that next. But yes, she started staying later, enjoyed her friends, and we didn't get to spend as much time together as we wanted to—having a baby is hard at any age, and it was hard on her with me busy. She wanted to keep working, and she did."

"Grandma kept me."

"As best she could. My mom, your Nanna, watched you a lot when you were first born until she got sick. Then we put you in day care a few times. Do you remember?"

Scarlet shook her head. "Not really. A little."

"Well, I started working at restaurants, too, after I finished my training, and when I was home I took care of you."

"Where was Mom?" Scarlet's voice was emotionless, but Patrick knew better and chose his next words carefully.

"Like I said, she made friends and enjoyed hanging out with them outside of work. I was a dreamer, a bit of an introvert. Always was. I liked staying home and being with you. We had different ideas about how we wanted to spend our time."

"But you started working at famous restaurants and leaving us alone." Her words were bitter and hurtful.

"No." Patrick kept his tone patient and firm. "She came home less and less, and I had to reach out to your grandparents more and more." He sighed. "Then one night, she didn't come home at all."

Scarlet held her breath, her fingers clutching the quilt on the side of the bed. After a quiet pause, Patrick continued. "A couple days later, your mom came to my parents' house with a police officer and took you away. It was a few days before I could get in touch with her, and she told me she didn't want to be married anymore." Patrick cleared his throat so his voice didn't crack. "I lived by myself in our apartment for a few months and every couple weeks I went out to your grandpa and grandma's trailer to see you."

"Why not Nanna?" said Scarlet. Her voice quavered. "Why couldn't I stay with you?"

"My parents wanted to help, badly, but your mother didn't want you around us."

"She said they tried to steal me."

"They did not," said Patrick calmly. "They wanted to help take care of you. You are their granddaughter as much as you are Grandpa and Grandma's."

Scarlet scrunched her mouth. "Why did you leave?"

"I wasn't allowed to see you, I didn't have money to go to court, and I didn't want to do that to your mom, or to you. When I heard about a job opening at my first big restaurant, I knew the experience and money would be great. And after the divorce went through, I had to make sure your mom had enough money to take care of you."

"Well, she didn't," said Scarlet sourly, then she caught herself. "I mean, she spent it. And she didn't have a job much." It was the first time Patrick had heard her speak the truth.

"Your mother never contacted me or returned my emails or calls."

"You sent toys."

Patrick flushed. "I'm glad you got some of them."

"I did at Grandma's house."

"Yes, I started sending them there to make sure." Patrick swallowed anxiously. He didn't want to criticize his ex-in-laws, but truth was truth. "Then they asked me not to send gifts anymore because they didn't have room."

"That doesn't make sense."

He sighed. "I don't really know, but they've had a hard time keeping up."

"They're sick a lot. And they don't have much.

I tried to help." Scarlet's voice cracked. "Sometimes Mom would come back and take me into Miami for a few days and then I stayed longer and longer there...and Jax came."

"Did it get better then?"

"Some, but it was still hard. He was tiny and sweet, and I took care of him."

"You did a great job. And you helped your mom out the best you could, but that wasn't your responsibility. She was supposed to take care of you."

"Why did you wait so long to come get us?"

"I didn't know," said Patrick. "Not until a social worker called. I didn't know she was leaving you alone or about the drugs...any of those things."

"My door had a lock," said Scarlet softly. "In the apartment. I kept it locked. I kept Jax with me and locked it when people came over."

"You did the best you could. I'm proud of you."

Scarlet searched his eyes. Patrick wrapped an arm around her shoulders without thinking, and she stiffened but didn't pull away. "You're not what happened to you. You are not your mom, and you're not me. You're brave and smart and talented in the arts, and baking."

"Baking?"

He grinned. "Your cupcakes sold in two days."

She released a soft chuckle as if she didn't believe him. "I really liked decorating them."

"Makes sense," he said. "I've seen your work."

"Dad?" The word warmed his heart. He inclined his head, encouraging her to go on. "Can I skip summer school suspension this Saturday to finish the mural?"

"I'm afraid not," he said reluctantly. "Mr. Abbot has seen your work, too." When she did not laugh at his little joke, he added, "Tam is going to make arrangements for you to do it during the weekdays next week."

"But the Flavor Festival is that weekend, and I babysit Jax on Mondays, Wednesdays and Fridays."

He smiled at her. "I can babysit if it comes to that. You'll get it done. There's plenty of time."

"Well, I do like the allowance. And Tam is going to pay me." Scarlet smiled at last.

"You're going to have a lot of savings in time to buy new school clothes," Patrick pointed out.

Her eyes brightened. "I've never had new clothes at the start of school."

"I'm your father, and I'll help you with what you need, but you're going to be able to buy most of what you want by yourself. That's impressive."

"I can make it stretch," she said. "You won't have to get anything."

"I want to," Patrick said and gave her another squeeze. "It's good to learn how to make and manage money while you're young, but I'm still your dad, and it's my job."

Their eyes met, and seeing the deep relief and gratitude in her eyes, he fought the urge to plant a kiss on her forehead. "Your scars are yours to share whenever you're ready. No one can see them or has to unless you want them to, but don't hold them against everyone you meet." Scarlet looked away. "You are not alone in the world, honey. You still have family that loves you and knows what's important and right. We're going to raise you the best that we can, and you're going to do great things."

Her eyes flooded with tears that spilled over, and her hands flew to her face. Sobs made her shudder. Patrick sucked in a breath to keep from joining her, but his own tears streamed from the corners of his eyes. He held her tightly and let her cry it out, wiping his cheek with his shoulder discreetly and hoping she never knew how much her pain would be a part of him forever.

Patrick related what had happened with Scarlet that night before Tam left. She was happy they'd tackled the difficult subject, and she said nothing when Piper continued her quiet intermittent texting over the next few days. When she took her to work with her on Monday, she fought the urge to sneak over and see how things were going at the bakery. It wasn't like she didn't have plenty to do. The teas and teacups were ready. Certificates and permits hung behind the counter. The furniture was polished, floors waxed, and local framed art hung on the walls. Patrick had her scone order.

She decided to head over after lunch while Piper stretched out on the small sofa in the back office. Turning the business sign over to mark her return in a half hour, she crossed the street in the sunshine, feeling the heat of summer in full swing. The streets and flower planters would bake, too. But that meant her cold brews like hibiscus and lime would be popular. She was certain. She breezed into the bakery and found Patrick stacking bags of rolls on a wooden rack. Jax was balancing in the middle of the room by holding on to a baby walker, his feet encased in cute mini sneakers.

"Nice shoes," she said, and Patrick turned and smiled. "Thanks. It's his first pair. I can't believe he's pulling himself up now."

"Looks like he's about to walk."

He grinned. "I can't wait."

"You have no idea what you're in for," she teased. Her heart pinched as fleeting memories of Piper's first steps rushed to her mind. It was such a joy to watch a child grow. She shook herself mentally and fell out of the tree of wistfulness. Her arms had never felt emptier. "I just wanted to check on the scones."

Patrick strolled to the register and flipped open a book.

"You don't use an online calendar?"

"Yes," he said with a moan. "We have programs, spreadsheets, and all that stuff. It's different from what I used before, and I'm still learning the financial side of things, but Donna's been great. It's not my forte like yours."

"I'm happy for you." Tam *was* happy that Patrick and his family were here. She was glad the bakery would stay open. She'd let her competitive nature skew her perspective of the situation like a pair of ill-fitting glasses. Her heart flooded with another tender feeling, and she blinked to disguise the old, familiar emotion. It must be kept at bay. For the girls' sake. For the businesses'. For her own.

She sighed, studying him, and he glanced up for a moment, eyes curious before returning to his calendar. "I'm sure you want them to be fresh, so I'll deliver them Friday about noon, and you can keep them sealed or freeze them overnight and warm them up later."

"How long will they take to bake?"

He gave her the time.

"I'm glad I got my food handlers permit," she said. "How many days do you think I can keep them fresh?" He gave her his opinion. "That works. I guess I better head back over. I've hired a high school boy, Lee Ellsworth, and a college student for the summer, and we have some training to do before the festival."

"You're brave." He smiled. "I'm still hanging on to Gretchen and paying Scarlet a few days a week."

"How is Scarlet by the way?"

"Not a happy camper. Mr. Abbott wouldn't let her work a double shift this Saturday so she won't be free for the festival weekend."

"Oh no! I thought that was worked out."

"We had worked it out but hadn't run it by him."

"Did he say why?"

"Something about life's consequences not being negotiable."

"Hmm. He's not wrong."

"I don't know," said Patrick in a droll tone. "All it takes is a good lawyer sometimes."

She chuckled. "Scarlet will be fine. Maybe she can get up super early. Do you know when she can come over and work on the mural?"

"How about tomorrow? She's worried about getting it done."

Tam nodded. "Tomorrow's fine. And thanks

for the update. I'll be ready for the delivery Friday night and pop them in the fridge." She exhaled as she worked out how early she'd have to set her alarm in the coming days.

"You'll get there," said Patrick, reading her mind. "I used to work 2:00 a.m. to ten in the mornings."

"I can't imagine," she groaned. "But I brought this on myself."

"As soon as we get into a good routine, I can deliver them baked as needed before you open."

"Great. That changes everything! Are you ready for the festival then?"

He waved his arm around the room. "I'm trying to move product from the last three days, there are items in the freezer ready to go, and I have some dry ingredients already mixed. Friday and Saturday morning will be my busiest time."

"Well, good luck." Tam looked around the store. "I'm sorry you didn't get the bakery painted in time. I know you're not a fan of the pink."

"Everyone seems to love it," Patrick admitted. "It's fine for now." He arched a brow. "And besides, now I have an artist to help me out when she's done with your gig."

Tam chuckled. "I don't know what I'd do without these girls."

He winked. "I happen to know they feel the same way about you."

Heart glowing, Tam headed back over to the shop. "Why so shiny?" asked Piper, who was up from her nap and pricing jars of Ali's new honey crop.

"It's warm out."

"Mmm-hmm."

A blush rose in her cheeks as Tam strolled to the register. Her daughter was growing up, developing awareness and instincts. "I'm just excited for the festival. We're all good on the scone order. Everything I can do is done."

"Besides training the two helpers. A cute guy named Lee Ellsworth is next door."

"Oh! He's a bit early. Perfect." Tam tried to put back on her business cap. It wasn't easy with her daughter's hints about the baker across the street.

On Tuesday, Patrick hurried to the bakery with Scarlet after dropping Jax off at Ali's house. As soon as they arrived, Scarlet gave him a fleeting wave and rushed across the street. He didn't mind losing her to Petals and Pie. Finishing a mural at a local business was an enormous accomplishment for a girl not yet in high school. It seemed to rub Mr. Abbott the right way, too. Although he hadn't budged on her punishment, he'd given in to her pleadings to allow her to come in two hours earlier on Saturday so she wouldn't miss the entire festival. She was doing her time dutifully, knowing it was nothing compared to what could have happened. After murmuring his thanks to God, Patrick was struck by the thought that he probably wouldn't have to worry about Scarlet taking dark paths now. She'd already walked through fires by no fault of her own.

She was stronger because of it, no matter how much it pained him. He knew he was right when he told her she'd do great things. He just had to provide the tools and love she needed. With another rush of gratitude for Tam, and a fresh determination to take Principal Abbott's side, Patrick set to work focused on what he needed to accomplish until it was time to pick up his little boy. Just as he grabbed his keys, his phone beeped with a message from the realty company. As soon as he put down a deposit, the duplex was theirs.

Chapter Fourteen

Wednesday morning, Tam did a slow walk-through of the tearoom at sunrise as the rest of town dozed. The mural looked incredible. The two new part-time hires had been trained. The scones would be ready on Friday. With a sigh of relief, she crossed the threshold into The Gracious Earth. Piper and Scarlet were whispering at the register, not the least bit tired after a sleepover in Tam's bedroom. Tam pulled a folded check out of the front pocket of her jeans. "For you," she said to Scarlet with a grin.

Scarlet looked a little embarrassed but accepted it with a brave attempt at a smile. "Thank you."

"Aren't you babysitting today?"

"Dad's going to teach me how to make croissants, then take me back home."

"Wow," marveled Tam. "I don't think I'd be brave enough to try that."

"It's definitely a skill, but I'm learning."

"You're amazing."

She shrugged. "I'm better at decorating."

"Do you enjoy it?"

"I do. A lot. Especially getting paid for it, but I don't think I'd want to do it for a living." She stopped and her cheeks flushed. "I mean, it's okay."

Tam laughed. "It's fine. No one expects you to be a baker just because it's what your dad loves. Especially your dad."

"I know. He offered to pay half for art classes. Or anything," she added, and Tam could have sworn her eyes glimmered. "I was even thinking about trying horseback riding lessons."

Piper squealed. "Lucky!"

"That's pretty expensive, but you can make anything happen with a little prayer and hard work."

"I know." Scarlet became serious. "I never prayed or went to church before, but I like going. It makes me think, and I get new ideas."

"That's great. I hope you realize someday God's really there and loves you."

"I don't understand it all, but it feels right."

"You're amazing, and I love you. Also, the mural is fantabulous."

Scarlet blushed, speechless at Tam's praise.

"I would love to take horseback riding lessons but I never wanted to pressure you," Piper confessed.

"Well, as soon as you're fourteen, I can officially hire you, and you can start saving," Tam promised.

Piper looked at Scarlet and smiled. "Scarlet has a bank account already."

"That's wonderful," said Tam. "You and I will work on that this summer." She floated over to the window to examine the quiet street. Banners were fluttering from the lampposts and barricades waiting against the wall of a store next to the bakery, ready to block off the street on Saturday during the festival. Her pulse hummed with excitement.

In the bakery window, Patrick had hung a silver, white, and turquoise banner. There was a display of cake stands in different sizes. One held a two-tier birthday cake, another a large pie, others piles of pastries. She imagined they were units that had become too stale to sell but still looked pretty. A sign on the front door said, Grand Reopening. She assumed two taped magazine pages in the corner of the glass were from his article. Good for him. The community was just trying to give him a leg up, and she shouldn't have been so envious. Besides, there was always next month. Or the next. She wasn't going anywhere. Lagrasse had always been there for her.

A fluttering stream of gray smoke caught her

eye, and she glanced up at the sky. It wasn't a cloud. She followed the snaking streamer over the block back down to the back of the roof of the bakery. Her humming happiness stopped abruptly. Concern crept down her spine. Scarlet walked up beside her with a book under one arm. "What's that?"

"I'm not sure, but I…"

"Fire!" Scarlet gasped and flung open the front door so hard it crashed into the shelf behind it. Rather than scold her, Tam was on her heels and sprinted across the street. She didn't think to pull the girl back when she opened the door to the bakery, and a puff of acrid smoke made them both trip backward. A fire alarm was screeching.

"Daddy!" screamed Scarlet. She jettisoned forward again, but Tam caught her by the shoulder. "No. Wait. I'm sure he's outside if he's already here."

"No!" She tried to pull away. "Ms. Gretchen!"

Piper arrived and helped hold Scarlet back. "Call 911," Tam told the girls, tossing them her phone. She pulled the front of her shirt up over her face and dashed inside only making it as far as the register before her eyes began to burn. She took a deep breath, uncovered her mouth and shouted, "Gretchen! Patrick!" over the screaming alarm. Nothing. Unable to go any farther, she stumbled back outside where Scarlet was on her phone.

Piper's face was white. "Mom!" she cried. She threw her arms around her. "You shouldn't have gone in there."

"I know," Tam admitted. "It was just long enough to call out for them. You stay here." She darted around the block and into the alley behind it. No cars were parked behind the bakery. The Closed sign on the front door had meant just what it said, although Patrick seldom opened when he arrived early.

The smoke over the roof was growing thicker. Someone from another store came out into the alley filled with concern. "We called 911!" Tam shouted.

"Need help?"

"I don't think anyone's inside!" She prayed that it was true. Sirens echoed in the distance, and she thanked God the firehouse was only a couple blocks away. Then she remembered Evan Hollister was captain. Putting a hand to her heart, she ran back around to Loger Street again, passing the first big firetruck. The road was filled with curious onlookers and cars, the fire chief's fire command vehicle, and an ambulance. Pain and panic ripped through Tam's throat. She'd never prepared for something like this; she hadn't lost a family member, a best friend, or a home. Her tragedies had always been emotional or temporal. All the heartbreaks and hurt feelings in the world meant nothing compared to the loss of someone she loved. Her heart whomped in her chest. She could not bear to lose a friend or a man she cared about. Tam raced down the sidewalk into the crowd of firefighters just as flames broke through the roof. "Oh, no!"

Evan Hollister caught her by the arms as if he'd seen her coming. "The girls are across the street," he said in a loud voice, and she turned to see Piper and Scarlet in front of The Gracious Earth. They were white as sheets, Scarlet's hands clutching her mouth. "Who's inside?" Tam pleaded.

"They're looking. No one yet. It was closed."

"Sometimes Patrick comes in early to bake."

"They're looking," Evan repeated. "Go across the street."

She wanted to argue, but common sense prevailed, and she sucked in a gasp of oxygen to right herself. The neighboring businesses needed to be saved, too, but Patrick! Gretchen! Try as she might to be strong, tears escaped, and Tam swiped at them as she jumped the curb to her business and opened her arms to the girls.

Piper's arms circled around her, and Scarlet's body shook at her side. Pressing their foreheads together, she prayed harder than she had in ages.

No promises. No bribes. Just pleading from the depths of her soul. Piper's hair brushed the wetness off her cheeks as she looked up. When she glimpsed down the sidewalk, her heart leaped at the sight. Patrick was running toward them, his eyes wide and lips parted as if calling out.

"Thank You!" was all Tam could cry to heaven. She flew from the girls down the sidewalk and into Patrick's arms. A flash of something in his eyes before he caught her made her wonder whether she wanted to wrap him in her arms or be wrapped in his.

"Scarlet!" he gasped.

Tam pointed. "Scarlet's right here. The girls stayed with me all morning."

"Daddy!" The tender title made Tam's throat hurt worse. She stepped back as Scarlet rushed past her and buried herself in Patrick's arms. "You're okay!"

"Yes, and Jax is with Donna."

"Gretchen?" Tam panted.

"I'm opening today." Patrick clutched Scarlet tight. "I mean, I did. I just left for a few minutes to run to the store for egg substitute. I ran out and—" He stopped to breathe. His eyes swam with shock.

"It's going to be alright," Tam assured him. He held out an arm out for her to join them, and Tam burrowed into his chest with Scarlet beside her.

* * *

The next morning the old brick building steamed, and the stores on either side of it were soaked through. The neighboring businesses had been saved, and Patrick tried to find some relief in that, but the bakery was ruined. Inside anyway. He clutched his head and flopped back down on the polished table in Petals and Pie.

"It's okay, Dad," said Scarlet from beside him. She set down a cup of tea that smelled comforting. "Ms. Tam said to drink this. She'll be right back."

He sat up, reminding himself that he was the parent, and she didn't have to fix this, but her loving comfort meant the world. He reached out for her hand as she turned away. "Thank you, honey."

Another arm draped over his shoulder, and he looked as Tam sat down on the other side of him. "Donna is on the way over. Ali will keep Jax. I've closed the herb shop for a few hours, and Piper will handle the phones. Just like yesterday."

A part of his brain suggested he point out that she needed to get ready for the Flavor Festival tomorrow. It no longer mattered for him. His store was not destroyed, but he would miss the festival, and it would take months for repairs and renovations. Patrick's heart limped along like he was a broken man. He didn't have months. He had bills and a lease, and he needed a down payment for the rental, but he wouldn't have the income. Not for a house and a business. The room spun a little, and he reached for the teacup.

Scarlet sat back down across from him, a look of helplessness and dread on her face.

"It's going to be okay," Tam said in an attempt to soothe them both.

"I don't know," he whispered, glancing at Scarlet.

"Yes, it will be, Dad," said Scarlet. "It always is in the end. You got me and Jax. Ms. Donna let us live with her." She looked across the street. "The bakery didn't burn down. I can help."

"You don't have to. It's my fault for leaving the ovens on."

"Don't blame yourself," said Tam. "Donna is beating herself up because she didn't have the system checked, especially with the shorts in the wiring giving her glitches. The fire marshal will figure it out, and it'll go through insurance." She took a breath. "Scarlet is right. It will be fine in the long run."

Patrick nodded, knowing she was just trying to help and loving her for it. He did love her, he realized, but stopped himself from leaning over and kissing her for comfort, for hope…and for forgiveness for what he knew he had to do. Besides, Scarlet was here and didn't need to witness him leaving another woman. His children were okay, but the world had just crashed down around them again. No bakery. No hope.

Eyes tearing, he reached for Tam's hand and gave it a hard squeeze. "I don't know how we're going to be able to stay here," he admitted, the thought crushing his soul. Going back to the bakery wasn't an option, but the job in Miami was waiting if he changed his mind. Or so they'd promised. He groaned, searching Tam's beautiful, disappointed eyes. She sacrificed everything for Piper. She was her world, and she was right to do it. And now he had to do what was right for his children. His lips felt numb as he whispered, "At least I can likely still get a job in Florida."

Tam's body felt as cold as ice as she slogged through the door to the house behind Piper. It'd been the longest day ever. Donna had dropped them off something to eat at Petals and Pie while they finished interviews and paperwork with the authorities. The new employees were called and assured they were still on for the grand opening the next day, and several purchases were made by visitors in The Gracious Earth, who spent more time looking out the window at the bakery and yellow caution tape than shopping, but she still made some sales. It was at Patrick's expense, though.

The thought nauseated Tam, but at least she was feeling. She'd gone from shock to action and back to shock; but for some reason it was the few simple words from Patrick that had done her in. Quit Lagrasse. Move back to Miami. She'd almost cried out loud, her heart ripping at the thought of him and his children leaving. But all she'd managed to say was, "Don't worry about that right now. The important thing is you're safe." And that was the important thing.

"I'm going to take a bath," she told Piper as her daughter collapsed on the couch in front of the TV. "You rest, okay?"

"Sure, okay." She sighed. "Mom?"

Tam was already down the hallway. She'd loosed the gasket, and tears had started to drip. He couldn't leave. She loved him. She loved his children. He made her world brighter, a light that had unexpectedly appeared in her life. Patrick had shown her that daddies still cared, men still had honor, and that she could still fall in love.

The tears fell faster. Tam ignored Piper's call and hurried to the bedroom. She shut the door behind her and collapsed onto the bed with aching shoulders. She had tried everything to make things work between The Last Re-Torte and Petals and Pie; and it was because she hoped for something to work out between her and Patrick.

But here they were. The fire meant a delay for his dreams so he was going to have to return to Miami. Just like the last man she'd fallen for had chosen to move on; just like Piper's father had done after he realized what having a child—and a family—meant. But Patrick was leaving for a good reason. And that hurt more.

She began to cry and put a pillow over her head to muffle the sound. It just wouldn't be the same without Patrick, Scarlet and Jax. Piper had been upset until the girls started discussing texting and video chats. It was so easy for them to handle the thought they might be pulled apart, although she'd been blindsided.

"Mom?"

Tam jumped at the sound of Piper's voice. She'd almost expected it to be Scarlet. How dearly Tam wanted to love her. She already did. Every girl needed a father, but she needed a mom, too. Why else would God create families the way that He did?

"Momma, can I come in?"

She wiped her cheeks. "Yeah, just a minute." Tam saw her tearstained face in the dresser mirror and knew there was no hiding it—but Piper didn't need to know why, not the full truth anyway. It'd just make her feel bad, and worse, it would find its way back to Patrick. He didn't need to learn she'd fallen in love with him. "You take the cake," she murmured to herself, trying to make herself chuckle, but it did nothing. Her chest was a deep, dark pit. She opened the door. Piper studied her.

"What's wrong? Are you stress crying or are you upset that the Butlers are moving back to Florida?"

"We don't know that for sure," Tam muttered.

"He said there wasn't any choice."

"I'm sure Donna and he can work something out."

"But he needs a job."

"Piper!" Tam held up a hand to stop her, stung at her daughter's expression and regretting the tone she'd used. "I'm sorry. I'm tired and lying down instead of taking a bath."

"Okay." Piper looked hurt.

Tam sighed. "I'm as upset as you are that they're leaving."

Piper pulled back her shoulders. "Then let's help them. Scarlet likes it here. Mr. Butler wants to run the bakery. And we both want them to stay."

Tam shook her head helplessly. "What can we do? I have the new business and the herb shop. They certainly can't move in with us. It wouldn't be appropriate."

Piper stared, and Tam imagined she could see the wheels turning in her little class president's head. "Ms. Donna said they could stay with her as long as it took. So that's covered."

"And what am I supposed to do? Hire him to sell tea?"

"Why not?" Piper's face flowered into a smile. "You said half of what you wanted from Europe didn't come or isn't sold at an affordable price."

"So?"

"You need a baker." She grinned. "A pastry chef."

For a few seconds, Tam forgot to breathe. "I can't afford a full-time pastry chef."

"One of the boys you hired already backed out. And if you pay Mr. Butler what you were going to pay him plus what you were going to order, doesn't it all come out evenly?"

"I don't know," said Tam, refusing to let in hope. "I doubt I could pay him what he's used to."

"We always have good sales in the summer," Piper pointed out. "And where will all The Last Re-Torte customers get their bread? Peach pies. It'll be like he's renting our kitchen."

"Piper, I don't think our kitchen is big enough. It wasn't built for that."

"Then he'll just have to make do." She grinned.

"Isn't that what you always say? Make do until it comes true?"

Tam smiled at her. A hopeful door creaked open a few inches. "I suppose. I didn't know you were listening."

"I listen more than you think, Mom."

"You are going to be an incredible business owner someday—or manager. Whatever you decide to do."

Piper grinned. "I like the idea of management. I don't have any special talent, but I am a good student. And I can still help you with the herb shop. Lee and Scarlet can help Mr. Butler in the tearoom."

"Ah," said Tam, pointing at her. "Then what happens when the bakery is rebuilt, and he leaves? Assuming he would stay." Oh, how she wanted him to stay.

Piper dropped onto the bed. "By then you could have someone trained to take his place, or you could order your pies from the bakery like you planned to start with."

"So we'd get all their business while they're down," said Tam slowly.

"And that would help pay Mr. Butler so they can stay."

Tam's chest tingled as she began to work out solutions. A prayer she had the courage to utter made her feel light and at peace. She leaned over and held Piper in her arms. "I don't ever want to hear you say you don't have any talents again," she whispered in her ear. "You are amazing!"

Patrick heated up oatmeal for Jax, then sat at the table scanning the list of emails he had yet to answer. Messages from the Realtor, newspaper, fire marshal, and insurance company filled his inbox. He had phone calls to make. Appointments to set up. And a contract on a home to cancel. Just when God had given him a blessing, He'd taken it back. Like Patrick's career. His marriage. His daughter. Lagrasse, and…

Patrick watched his little boy try to shovel the gloppy oats into his mouth. He rubbed his forehead. Thank goodness Scarlet was still sleeping. Donna, too. The excitement had worn out his aunt, while Scarlet had withdrawn from the shock and heartbreak. He knew she didn't want to go back to Miami anymore. But she hadn't said a word. The rug had been pulled out from under her, too, and she'd autopiloted right back into survival mode. He suspected tears had been shed under her quilt last night.

At least Donna had urged him to take his time. He hated he was putting her out, but her suggestion to get a temporary job was tempting. He could bag groceries, wait tables, anything until the bakery was refitted, but he would still be under her roof, and the bakery would be losing business and loyalty, while debts stacked up. He sighed. There was no way he could make enough with a minimum wage job, not with his children.

Felix rubbed against his ankle, and he scooted back and picked up the cat and held him tight. As if sensing he was on the fringes of becoming unglued, the cat rumbled and rested his chin in the crook of Patrick's arm. Poor kitties. They'd grown accustomed to Donna's house and loved roaming in and out during the day. It wouldn't be right to drag them into a city apartment in the heat of Miami. But he couldn't leave them here.

Jax threw his spoon and grinned, signaling he was finished, and after quietly admonishing him, Patrick cleaned him up. Rather than rinse the dishes, he took the baby in his arms and let himself out the back door into the summer sunshine. It was just a few yards to the fence between the house and the peach orchard. Patrick pushed a gate open with his hip and walked in, noting another crop was ready to be collected. Thoughts of Tam shot rays of relief through his mind, and he imagined he heard her voice.

"Hey. Patrick?"

He turned in surprise, and Jax gurgled.

She chuckled. "I didn't mean to startle you."

"I didn't hear you."

"I was just getting ready to knock when

Donna opened the door. She was getting her newspaper."

"She's up now? Did she seem okay?"

"A little stiff," Tam admitted. "How's Scarlet?"

"Still sleeping. We were up most of the night again."

Tam walked over and looked up at the trees. Patrick let Jax slip down into the grass. He promptly pulled himself up using the tree trunk.

"Any day now."

"And?"

"He'll be running all over the place."

"It feels like he already is."

She smiled, and he looked away when their eyes met. But he could still feel her watching. Searching. For what? What could he offer her? He couldn't even take care of his own kids. And he didn't know if she felt the same way.

"You aren't still blaming yourself, I hope."

"I should have turned the ovens off. It doesn't matter about the wiring. I knew better."

"You had no idea that would happen. People step out for a few minutes all the time when they have a long bake."

"You've baked bread?"

"Oh, no," said Tam, and she burst out laughing.

"What?"

"I can't even get bread dough to rise. I make good cookies, though."

"You have a great palate," he said.

"Really?"

"Your tea blends are delicious. Original."

"Oh, thanks." She smiled. "I help Ali with her beeswax products sometimes."

"Art is not all paint, clay, and wordplay." He smiled. "It's anything you love and do well."

"I have to agree. Any idea how long the bakery repairs will take?"

He shook his head. "No. I haven't even started on that, but with water and smoke damage I assume it will be gutted."

"What about the freezer?"

"What about it?"

"Was it damaged?"

"Not that I know of. Why?"

"I was thinking we should get over there today and get everything out that hasn't thawed."

Patrick blinked in surprise and drew in a breath of peach-laced air. "I hadn't thought that far ahead."

"It was Piper's idea," Tam admitted. "She can work out things pretty well for a teenager."

"She's quite the young lady. But what would I do with it all? And where would I put them?"

Tam put a finger to her chin as if thinking, then chuckled. "I called Pizza Pies, and they said they have storage room for you. Ali has an extra freezer, and I have the small one in Petals and Pie. Between the three of them, I think we can save a lot of your work."

"That'd be great," said Patrick. "But I'm not… I mean…"

Something flitted over her face, and Patrick's heart dropped to the ground. "Tam, I'm not sure that I'm staying. I have to think things out, to pray about it for sure."

"I just want you to know everyone is willing to help you out if you ask, and they are already praying for you. I know I am."

"You are?" He smiled at her.

"Of course I am."

He wished she wasn't so many inches away but knew it was best. "We want you to stay, Patrick," she continued. "I want you to stay. I mean, the whole town does. Piper and Scarlet especially. Don't jump ship too soon."

He smiled wryly at her. "I waited too long to get back to my daughter. I just want to act fast on her behalf."

"You can act fast," said Tam. "You can start tomorrow."

"Doing what?"

"Making my scones." He laughed, but the suggestion stung a little. She was still thinking about her grand opening when his was ruined?

"I'm sorry," he said. "I have more important things to think about."

"You think I'm thinking about myself, don't you?"

Patrick bit back a guilty smile.

"Patrick Butler, I'm offering you a job."

He arched a brow, then crossed his arms over his chest. Jax babbled something that sounded like he was explaining, too. "A job doing what? I can get a job, it's what kind of job that matters."

"You'd be baking, and I'll meet your salary that Donna provided when you arrived until you bought the bakery. My order of pies from Atlanta came in this morning, but you could stay as pastry chef at Petals and Pie. Scarlet can help whenever she wants. I'll fill in as needed."

"You want me to take over Petals and Pie during your grand opening?"

"Why not? It'll give you a chance to show everyone what you can do, and they'll all have questions about the fire. It'll be *the* place to be, to get the local gossip and news."

He stared at her, incredulous. "How are you going to manage all these salaries?"

"As long as we can cover yours and the rent on the store's space, I'm not really losing any money here."

He stared at her in amazement. He could still bake. He could oversee the bakery's repairs, and best of all, he might be able to keep his family in Lagrasse. With Tam… No. It was all a dream. He couldn't do all that and find a home, too. The job in Miami would be a sure thing. "But I'd get all the glory."

"Glory, shmory. I'm still owner. Besides, it's what neighbors do. And friends."

"Friends," he repeated. This was more than friendship. He knew it. She wanted him to stay. And she knew it. They were good together. But could he tell her he loved her? It'd all happened so fast.

"Look," he said, heart rending because it needed something he couldn't have. "I'll take care of Petals and Pie this weekend. I can commit to, let's say, two weeks," he offered. That should give him time to discuss things with the restaurant in Miami. To make a decision. He couldn't put his heart first right now.

"You'll stay."

"I doubt it. I've already heard back from the restaurant folks that they're interested in talking."

"I'm so glad, I mean…" Tam trailed off. "Piper will be disappointed."

"Will you?" he asked before he could stop himself.

She studied him for a long time under the heavy branches of the peach tree, then seemed to come to a decision when she transferred her gaze to Jax. "Oh, look," she cried, crouching to the ground. Jax toddled across the grass with a cry of excitement, straight into her arms.

Patrick's eyes teared again, but this time with joy at seeing his son take his first steps. At least that's what he told himself. The Lord had opened a window. He just had to pick up the pieces. Miami wouldn't be so bad. And now he had time to get ready. There was only one person who could change his mind, but he had to do what was best for all of them.

Chapter Fifteen

How could it be the first weekend in June already? Tam sighed with contentment as she let herself into The Gracious Earth. Lagrasse was a rainbow of summer colors. Petunias, salvia, coneflowers, and red roses flowered the landscape beneath the Georgia pines. She wondered how much longer it would be before the blueberries were ready. She only had six bushes in her backyard, but they produced wonderfully for being situated on a small property in town. Someday, on her own land, she could have an entire orchard if she wanted. If her shops flourished like the flora and fauna around her. Instead of herbs, the smell of baking bread washed over her when she opened the door. It filled her with instant peace that was quickly replaced with a yearning, but not for food. Patrick was here.

She blinked, pushing her emotions to the back of her mind, locking them up where they belonged. She forced herself to focus on the task at hand, the monumental achievement she'd been working toward for so many months. She scanned the herb shop for anything out of place, straightened a sale sign over Ali's honey jars, then strode through the breezeway into the tearoom next door. The front lights were still off, but the ones over the register were on. Behind it and down the hall, the kitchen glowed and something within clattered. She took a deep breath and walked around the corner.

"Oh, hi, Ms. Tam," said Scarlet brightly. She looked up, her fingers curled around a pastry bag squirting white icing.

Patrick straightened from her double oven, a powdery dark blue apron fitted around his waist. "Good morning."

"Something smells delicious."

"It's the scones."

"Where's Jax?"

"Gretchen has him this morning. I'm picking him up after the festival."

"That was nice of her."

"Her girls were excited to play with him."

"I bet. I'll miss him today."

"Me, too," said Scarlet more to herself. "Where's Piper?"

"She had trouble getting up this morning so she's going to ride her bike down in a bit. Did you clean at the school today?"

"Yes, the principal let me come in before it even got light."

"Wow, you must have been up early."

"She was," said Patrick, which meant he must have been exhausted. "How busy do you think this festival will be today?" Patrick turned to slice a pie.

"Hundreds," said Tam. "It usually peaks around late morning through lunchtime."

"That's exciting." He sounded like he was trying to stay optimistic.

"It should be. I'm sure we'll have a lot of questions about the bakery."

"That's okay," said Scarlet from her workstation. "Piper and I have already worked out the story."

"Have you?" Tam chuckled.

"Yes, can I go over to the herb store and help when I'm done here?"

"If it's okay with your dad."

Patrick nodded.

"Lee Ellsworth should be here soon," said Tam.

Patrick gave Scarlet a sideways glance. "Scarlet's looking forward to meeting him."

"I am not," she said, a little too hotly. Tam laughed.

Scarlet insisted, "I just wondered who he was."

"Because he's in high school?"

"Not really," Scarlet said coolly.

Tam chuckled again. "I'm sure it has nothing to do with the fact Piper thinks he's cute."

Patrick arched a brow, and Scarlet concentrated profusely on what she was doing.

"I'll be back to open and get Lee settled at the register." He nodded, and Tam returned to her other store, heart seesawing between happiness and sadness that they might go away again.

Within a half hour of opening, the streets began to crowd as vendors set up on sidewalks and around the park. A band played music from a temporary grandstand down the block, and it floated along the breeze. Visitors came and went. They tasted honey, accepted essential oil samples, browsed vitamins and herbs, and several bought bags of herbal teas. Many others wandered next door eager to try a cup and have a piece of pie or scone.

Tam tapped out when Ali arrived, all smiles, with more honey stick samples. Piper skipped to catch up with Tam and walk over to check on the tearoom. It was busier than the herb shop and much more crowded. Lee was at the register, having no problems thanks to his past experience working fast food; Patrick was refilling trays on the counter with delectable pastries.

When Scarlet waved, Piper joined her, and Tam called for her to grab a hair net and rewash her hands. Patrick grinned at her on his way back to the kitchen. She sent him a smile and grabbed a spray bottle and towel to wipe down a table—Scarlet's job. But she was distracted, and Tam let her be. She glanced at Lee and sighed. Heartbreak was a part of life; but she couldn't resist the idea of having a word with him. She wanted to prevent the girls from getting their hearts broken for as long as possible.

"Tam!" Her mood soared at the tone of Kylee's voice. She had both sets of her twins with her, and Ali was sitting with Jax on her lap at a long table with Donna and Gretchen. Heath had found a corner chair and was holding Alice. Monk and Angie Coles from church were at a table for two.

"Hello, everyone," called Tam. They all held up their drinks—smoothies, cold tea brews, a chilled latte—and cheered. She laughed. "Thank you for coming in."

"It's great to have somewhere to meet up," said Ali.

Kylee added, "And not have to buy a big meal."

"Especially with the bakery down," noted Heath.

Tam nodded. "Well, you can get your pastries here."

Donna smiled. "I'm glad you gave him a job, although I'd hate to see the bakery close for good."

"You can't make his decisions for him, Mom," Gretchen reminded her. Tam knew Gretchen was right. Patrick had to live his life, and that meant deciding whether or not to let the bakery go. She should have learned her lesson. Falling in love meant heartbreak for Tam Rochester. But at least she and Patrick could always be friends.

"Sit down for a moment," said Kylee, likely sensing Tam's fatigue and sadness.

Tam sat quietly and laid the towel across the table. Donna mentioned her favorite kettle corn vendor was at the corner. A jazz band from Atlanta would be playing in the late afternoon in the last slot. The room hummed with conversation, music, and the occasional outburst of laughter. Tam crossed her legs and bounced her leg. It was nice.

This is where she was supposed to be. Besides, Florida was too hot, too far, and she hadn't been invited.

She watched the door swing open and the line grow long. Giving Kylee a hug, Tam then hurried to the register to help fill cups with hot water and to-go bags with pastries for happy, chattering customers.

It wasn't the formal Southern tearoom she'd first envisioned, but it was the type of place Lagrasse really needed, and more importantly, it was filled with people she loved and friends she wanted to get to know better.

Patrick kept the baking case stuffed. Starved, Tam took a slice of pie, then set it on the counter for people to watch her eat. Why not let them see she enjoyed a tasty treat as well as a mug of peach tea? A newspaper reporter asked for her business card and if she'd be open to doing a story about her festival experience. She told the story about discovering the fire about seven times. The hours whirled by, and finally, the steady stream of visitors petered out as the band at the park wrapped up, the sounds of smooth jazz fading away. Scarlet disappeared back into the herb shop, where Tam assumed she and Piper would be giggling in the office about Lee.

Tam's feet ached, but she'd loved every minute of it. Her friends had made her new vision a reality. She knew in her heart this business would succeed and that her daughter's future was secure. She just didn't know what would become of her heart.

Patrick wiped around the sink, checked the counters for crumbs again, and sent up a prayer of thanksgiving that tomorrow was the Sabbath and both Tam's businesses remained closed on those days. The grand opening had been an incredible success. She'd been smart to open on a festival day.

Patrick didn't bother to obsess over the ruins across the street. There was nothing he could do about it. No one had betrayed him. No one had lied, cheated, or kept him in the dark. It'd been something beyond his control. And why God had let it happen, he'd understand someday. Just like he understood now why he'd been led to La-grasse. He had his daughter back.

He came around the corner as he untied his apron. Lee had left. The tearoom was quiet. The girls had disappeared. It was like the bakery at closing time, but softer, cozier. Tam was sitting at one of the tables staring out the window. She turned when she heard him come up beside her and climbed to her feet. "Hey."

"Caught you woolgathering."

"You must be exhausted."

He shook his head. "I'm no stranger to twelve-hour days."

"I am." She chuckled. "Today was crazy. I'm going to have to hire more help."

"I suspected as much. But that's a good thing."

"Yes, I know. I can't count on Ali and the girls to take up the slack forever."

"You can count on me." It came out before he could stop himself. He searched her blue eyes.

"Can I?" she said softly. "Or just until you go?"

Patrick resisted the urge to throw his arms around her, then realized he'd been resisting the urge too long and for all the wrong reasons. Leaving Lagrasse might give him a job, but at what cost when he could try to make things work here?

"If we do well enough, I could… I mean, I ran the numbers," he babbled. "I could stay in town. Get the rental. Make things work until the bakery is back up and running. It'd be tough, but it's doable."

"Then why not?" Tam' eyes searched his. "Why are you insisting on leaving?"

"I guess…" He cleared his throat. "I guess a part of me wanted to go because of the risks I'm taking if I stay."

"What risks? We have you covered."

He took a deep breath. "There's still my heart. It's vulnerable. I forgot what that felt like. How scary. But look at Scarlet. She's handling it."

Tam stilled, and Patrick wondered if he was doing the right thing. Her words would be the deciding factor. Miami would be familiar to him and his kids. It was once home, and it could be again; but was that the home he wanted? He didn't want to be there without Donna, Gretchen, and his new friends. But mostly— without Tam. But he didn't want to stay and not have her, either.

"Tam," he said, voice deepening. He reached for her hand. "You've done a lot for me, and I appreciate that."

"Me?" She laughed, but it was a painful sound, and she pulled away. "You've made my grand opening a whopping success. I couldn't have done it without you. Not to mention…" Her voice faded. "You've shared Scarlet with us. Piper has a best friend—a real best friend. She's always had big circles, she's never really had a close one. It was always me and her, and well, she needs friends her own age," Tam admitted. "I see that now. We'll miss Scarlet."

There. She'd answered his question. She was okay with letting him go. It stung, but Patrick had no intention of taking it home. She deserved to know, just like his daughter should have known all along that—

"I love you," he blurted. Her eyes rounded in shock. "Before I leave, you need to know that I care for you, and I don't want to go." He touched his chest. "My heart says stay. But my head says do what's best. For everyone."

Tam's eyes flooded with tears, and she raised her hand as if she wanted to touch his cheek, but it hung there, wavering. "Patrick, I want you to stay."

But? He held his breath. Could he bear working across the street from a woman he'd fallen in love with?

"I…" She stiffened, and he cringed, seeing business mode all over her face. "But it's not for the bakery, and it's not for the children."

He blinked in surprise. "I mean it is," she admitted as if embarrassed by his reaction, "but in this moment and situation, I need to do what's best for me." She touched her heart. "For my life. Not my business. Not anyone else." She took a deep breath. "I think… I loved you from the first moment you opened your door covered in cats."

"You did?" He laughed, relief and happiness buoying his courage with her words. He'd waited, praying for the tide to turn his way. He'd been waiting so long.

"Stay," she whispered. "Let me love you. Let me love your children."

Joy trickled through him, but still unsure, he ordered himself to let go—take off the mooring, the reservations and be happy and believe again. "If there's anyone I could have that with, I know it would be with you." He wagged his head in disbelief. "I'll stay," he assured her. "There's nothing more important to me—not a bakery, not a dream." He smiled at her as a single tear escaped, and he let it go. Tam's fair cheeks were ruby red.

"Congratulations to Petals and Pie," he said

softly. He reached out and put a finger under her chin, drawing her near to him. "You're the dream." And he kissed her, soundly, knowing that not only were his feet firmly planted but his heart—and family—had finally found the woman and roots they could call home.

Epilogue

Patrick leaned back on his arms on the blanket beneath a big peach tree watching autumn-frayed leaves twirl through the air before they hit the ground. From the other side of the orchard, Jax screeched in delight as he ran from Piper. Scarlet sat off to the side sketching them. Her hair was cut short, just above the ears, with long tufts of raven locks flopped at an angle across her crown. She looked like a mischievous pixie except for the razor-cut jeans and royal blue Art Club T-shirt.

He smiled to himself and reached into his pocket, tapping his fingers. No one knew but her. Jax was only fourteen months old, but his vote would have been obvious. Jax held his arms up to Tam, who put away her camera and reached over Piper to steal the toddler. Piper plopped down beside her friend to look out over the orchard Patrick had bought from Donna. His godmother had moved into her own small apartment behind Gretchen's house in September. There was no need to put the farmhouse up for sale. He broke his lease with the rental in town and moved back in with his children. And yet, as happy and at home as they felt, it still didn't feel quite complete. A long, lingering kiss of congratulations from Tam on the front porch steps after the housewarming party she'd thrown for him had put a period at the end of the sentence he had been waiting for. She was supportive after he reopened the bakery, happy for him for buying a home, and she loved him. Best of all, she treated his children like her own. This one, he could not let get away. And he knew it the minute he walked into the housewarming with Scarlet, grinning like the Cheshire cat beside her.

Tam hauled a wiggling Jax back to the blanket and sat down beside him. The baby rolled off her lap to stare at the trees overhead. She looked up. "They'll be bare soon. Then where are you going to hang out?"

He leaned over and brushed a kiss across her cheek. "At Petals and Pie. Where else?"

She laughed. "You're always welcome there. Anywhere."

"Good." He smiled. The girls had bowed their heads over something Scarlet had sketched. A whispering breeze bent the yellowed grass blades of the orchard over as if encouraging them to settle in for the winter to come. He shivered.

"It's going be a lot cooler here than in Miami," Tam warned.

"That's no problem for me," he assured her, searching her beautiful eyes. "We do have a fireplace, and I like getting cozy."

She blushed, but chuckled. "You have two cats to keep you warm."

He took a deep breath, prepping himself for the conversation he'd put off for weeks. The question hung like the whisper of winter on the wind. "It may be time for you to consider getting allergy shots," he suggested. He swallowed when she looked at him in surprise. "Or, Scarlet and I may have to let Felix and Jasmine go. Donna is open to taking them."

"I can't ask you to do that!" Tam exclaimed. "We have an unspoken truce that neither one of us will bother the other, and I'm not here enough to be utterly miserable."

"I don't want you to ever be miserable, and I want you here all the time."

She smiled at him, and the love in her eyes boosted his courage. "An antihistamine works fine before I come over."

He reached into his pocket again. "Well, how much would you have to take if you stayed over?"

She looked at him in surprise. "What do you mean?"

"I mean, do you think you could be happy here outside of town? And Piper, too?" He motioned to the field behind the orchard. "There's an acre of land back there just begging to be tamed. I hear lavender grows well around here."

She stilled, one brow rising, and he saw her throat ripple with a nervous swallow. "What do you mean, Patrick? You know I've always wanted to expand my garden." She stopped with a sudden intake of breath.

He reached for her hand and put it over his heart. "I mean that…" He took a gulp of breath and fumbled for the wedding ring he'd been carrying around in his pocket for weeks. Then he pulled out the rare blue diamond that was as close to the colors of her eyes as he could find. He held it out by the platinum band. "I brought you an offering." Her eyes widened, and he remembered to get on one knee like his daughter had instructed him because real love "was not lame."

"I brought you my heart—on a platter." He held out the ring again. "This comes with it, and it's yours to keep no matter what you decide. A gift from me and my children."

Tam's eyes flooded with tears, and her hands

went to her mouth. She ducked her head and laughed. "Oh, you!"

"Marry me, Tam."

She jumped to her feet and pulled him up with her, dancing around Jax so they didn't step on him. She took a deep breath, and it felt like an eternity until she answered—as long as it'd taken for him to find her, see her, trust her. A mother for his children. A love for himself. "Will you marry me? Be my partner and friend forever?"

"Yes." She nodded, hands clasped over her mouth and tears streaming from her gleaming eyes. She let out a nervous giggle. "With or without that stunning ring, but yes!"

His face stretched into a smile that healed everything behind him and prepared him for what was ahead. "I love you, Tam Rochester."

"I love you, too," she choked, then took the ring and threw her arms around his neck.

"Finally!" cried Piper.

Laughing through his own tears, Patrick turned to see the girls a few feet away watching with glossy expressions.

"Gross," teased Scarlet, sketch pad dangling in her hand. "We don't need the mental image, Dad."

"Dadda!" cried Jax at Patrick's feet. He and Tam released each other and reached down to pick him up at the same time. They straightened and gave him a double squeeze. "And let's talk about downsizing three businesses," Tam pleaded from over the baby's head. "Piper has a nest egg now, and I don't think I could take on three stores with three children."

He grinned at her. "Deal." And leaned in for another kiss.

"Group hug!" shouted Piper, and she dashed over and wrapped her arms around them. Patrick looked up and extended an arm for his daughter. For one brief moment, Scarlet hesitated, then she shook her head in theatrical disgust and mumbled, "Lame," before hurrying over and wrapping her arms around her family.

* * * * *

Dear Reader,

Thank you for joining me in Lagrasse to meet new characters once more. This is the third book set in this fictional town inspired by LaGrange, Georgia. From the start, I wanted to do something fun with the bakery, because who doesn't like pie? There is nothing more lovely or sweet smelling than the peach orchards in Georgia, and although the fruit took a back seat, I wanted to incorporate this time of year and our traditional Southern hand pies with this blended family story.

Just as Tam and Patrick had experienced, sometimes first love doesn't last, or people make mistakes. Regardless, everyone deserves loving parents and a loyal partner at their side. Families are forever, whether they are formed by blood or life bonds.

I hope you enjoyed Tam's journey in finding love for herself and a family for her daughter. Second chances can be hard to take! Don't let that hold you back. All my gratitude to the editors and staff at Love Inspired who bring my stories to life, and most importantly, thank you for reading my books and supporting inspirational romance.

Warmly,
Danielle Thorne